Caleb Barnes was a gambler who didn't pay his debts. And Gunn had warned him of his chances in an impatient town. In the end, Caleb lost more than a game of cards: He lost his life, and he left Gunn with a full hand—Caleb's daughter. Debbie was a strong girl, but her father's death and two long days on the road with Gunn took their toll:

"Hold me, Gunn. Hold me tight. I can't stop shaking."

Gunn felt her breasts flatten against his chest. When her face brushed against his, moments later, he tasted the salt of her tears. Boldly, he grasped her chin, tilted her face up to his. He kissed her hard on the lips, his manhood straining against the confinement of buckskin.

"I'll make us a bed," she husked.

"Yeah," Gunn rasped. "You better. This ground is getting awful hard."

FIRST-RATE ADVENTURES FOR MEN

AN
ADULT
WESTERN

THE HOTTEST NEW WESTERN SERIES!

TRIAL BY SIXGUN

GUNN

BY JORY SHERMAN

ZEBRA BOOKS
KENSINGTON PUBLISHING CORP.

DEDICATION

For Patrick and Jaqueline
who ride the Blue Horse.

ZEBRA BOOKS

are published by

KENSINGTON PUBLISHING CORP.
475 Park Avenue South
New York, N.Y. 10016

CHAPTER ONE

The land had a heartbeat to it.

Atop the big dun, Gunn listened to the horse's gait eating up the miles, hooves pounding on a hard-packed trail. It was good to be moving again, far from Taos, away from the stench of Santa Fe, the Gallinas mountains in the distance, the Rio Grande a shimmering ribbon under a cloudless blue sky. The new dun under him, stepping proud as his regal name, Duke. The horse was a gift, from Soo Li who was well on her way to San Francisco by now. The parting had been a rough thing, tearful on her part, heart clutching on his. To see her again, then have to wave goodbye . . . well, it was a hard thing to do. But Soo Li had her life, he had his. And there had been other women since Laurie, all of them a blur now in his mind, the country reaching out for him swallowing him up, blotting out memories with its insistent heartbeat.

The wagon appeared abruptly.

It was barely moving.

Gunn drew up, hauling hard on Duke's reins.

Something was damned sure wrong.

A lone wagon way out there in the big emptiness.

Just creeping along. Like some wounded beast.

"Steady now, Duke." The horse was becoming accustomed to its name. He had no idea what it had been called before, but it was no Mexican horse. It had been broke right, gelded neat as a foal. Duke had at least three good gaits, could probably go to five in time. Now, the horse stood there impatiently switching its tail, hip-shot, not even breathing hard. The morning air was crisp and Gunn could smell the river, almost feel its liquid pulse.

Duke's ears perked as it spotted the slow-moving wagon, its two oxen plodding along.

Duke nickered low.

Gunn patted its neck. The saddle creaked with his weight.

The wagon stopped.

Five hundred yards away.

Gunn saw no sign of movement. But someone was surely sitting there, watching him. Not outside the wagon's covered bed, but inside. It was a Conestoga, canvas or duck covering the bed. Carrying a load from the way the oxen pulled, the look of the springs.

Duke sniffed the air, pawed the ground with a forefoot.

"See anything, boy?"

Gunn slipped the thong off the hammer of his Colt .45. Dried his palm on the side of his buckskin shirt. He didn't look for trouble, nor expect any, but one couldn't be too careful in wild country. The Santa Fe Trail had its share of violence and a lone wagon was enough of an oddity to make any man suspicious.

He stood up in the stirrups, surveyed the land around him. He saw no sign of man beyond the silent covered wagon.

The tall man with the blue-gray eyes tapped Duke's flanks with his rowelless spurs. Flapped the reins against the horse's neck.

Duke trotted toward the wagon, nostrils distended. He shied at every stately saguaro, every barrel cactus until Gunn had to speak to him, pull the bit back hard against his mouth to keep him headed in the right direction. The horse sidestepped the clumps of brittlebush, the guayules growing near the saguaro. His hooves crushed lechugilla and the narrow-leafed sotol, as it made its way off-trail, to come up behind the wagon.

The wagon was two, three hours out of Socorro, Gunn figured, heading for Las Cruces. It had wandered off the trail, whether by design or accident, he didn't know. The oxen didn't appear thirsty. If they had thirst, they might have bolted toward the Rio Grande, or at least made their needs known by pulling at the traces. Instead, the two oxen stood there, heads bowed, weary, as if unable to plod another step.

Beyond the river, Gunn saw dunes of dazzling white sand, gypsum. He knew what gypsum was. The sawbones used it to make plaster of paris. Artists, too, he reckoned. In New Mexico, there was plenty of it, if one wanted to face the murderous Apaches. Over there, the yuccas stood, out of bloom now, sentry posts for quail.

Gunn circled the wagon, his bronzed face a mask that looked as if it had been hammered in bronze as the sun beat down on it from the west. There was no one on the seat of the wagon and the canvas was drawn tight. Once he thought he heard a low moan, but he couldn't be sure. The reins were wrapped around the brake loosely, but the brake was off. Yet something, or someone, had surely halted the wagon.

He rode around to the rear, more cautious than before. He made a wide circle, his right hand dangling near his pistol.

"Hello the wagon," he called softly, when he was about fifty yards away.

There was no answer.

No sound.

He watched the canvas to see if it moved.

Nothing.

"Anybody in there?" he called again, Duke stepping out in a slow canter toward the wagon.

More silence and the earth seemed to take a breath.

When it came, Gunn wasn't ready.

Not by a damn sight.

The snout of a pistol poked through the canvas just above the wooden backboard.

He sucked in a breath, made his right hand into a claw.

"You mean to shoot?" he asked. "I'm just riding through."

A face appeared, framed by the canvas as the drawstring was loosened. He saw her then, a young girl. A woman, perhaps. Dirt and tears streaked her face. He saw part of the faded dress, torn at the bodice so that one of her breasts showed white as a honeydew melon. Dark curly hair, pale blue eyes, delicate shoulders. She squinted over a bruise on her left cheek, as she aimed down the barrel of the pock-barrel .32 Smith. The barrel was shiny where it had lost its bluing, pitted from age and rust.

The pistol could kill just the same.

Kill him dead.

"Haven't you done enough to us?" asked the girl. The woman.

"Huh? Never saw you before in my life." Gunn drew a breath. "Honest."

The .32 Smith was cocked.

Sweat oozed out of the pores on Gunn's sun-bronzed face.

Something was damned sure wrong here. The girl was scared, but she was ready to squeeze the trigger. Blow him to kingdom come and then some. He could almost feel her finger tighten on the trigger.

"Ain't you one of Nat Larrabee's men?"

Gunn let out his breath.

"Hell no. Never heard of him, either. I'm a stranger here, lady, and if you'll put that pistol down I'll listen to your trouble."

A low, agonizing moan came from inside the wagon.

The girl turned, disappeared along with the pistol.

Gunn rode up cautiously, swung down out of the saddle. He hitched Duke up to a wheel, looked inside. It was dark. The girl was bent over something. Something white, feathered. The moans came from there.

"Can I help, Miss?"

The girl jumped, startled.

9

"Oh, please. My pa. He's in a bad way."

"Let me take a look."

The girl moved to one side. The white feathered thing groaned, tried to sit up. Gunn saw a rawhided face, the mouth move. The object was not recognizable as a human being at first. Gunn peered intently into the wagon, saw that it was indeed a man.

Tarred and feathered.

A low curse escaped Gunn's lips.

"What happened to you, man?" he asked. "Who in hell did this to you?"

"He—he can't talk much," said the girl. "He's my pa, Caleb Barnes. I'm Deborah, his daughter."

"Debbie," croaked her father, stretching out a feathered arm.

"Yes, Pa. I'm here."

"Help me, for God's sake, help me." The anguish in the voice was unmistakable. The pain. The man fell back, exhausted with the effort at speech. He smelled of chicken feathers and tar.

Gunn shook his head.

The man would die if he didn't get that tar off his skin. The pores were clogged up and his breathing was shallow. The tar was like an iron corset, suffocating him.

"We've got to get him to the river," Gunn said. "Fast."

He'd seen tar and feathers before. A long time ago, when he was a boy growing up near Osage Creek in Arkansas. And again, during the War when a town coated three men with hot tar and rolled them in a heap of chicken feathers. One of these men

10

had died from the shock, another had gone crazy. The third had strangled on his own vomit. He would never forget the sight of any of those men. The first man, in Arkansas, had been caught stealing money from an elderly widow. He was not a local man. Tar and feathers had been applied and the man ridden out of town on a hickory rail, the crowd jeering and taunting him all the while. He had been dumped in the woods, naked except for his suit of pitch and feathers. Months later, he had been seen in Fort Smith, his skin raw as a plucked bird's and he had to leave that place in a hurry when folks spotted him.

Debbie Barnes drove the wagon to the bank of the Rio Grande, Gunn following on Duke.

"You get some big pots and haul water while I get a fire going," Gunn told her. "This is going to take some time."

He hoped it would work, too.

Somewhere he had heard that the only sure way to get the tar off was to heat it again with hot water and scrape it off. It was slow work and painful as hell, but it was better than dying in agony. Maybe.

Gunn stacked up piles of brush, ranging far to gather enough fuel to get a hot fire going. Sweat soaked through his buckskins until finally he skinned out of his shirt. He used cow pies and buffalo chips too, dried to hard cakes by the baking sun.

Debbie filled two large pots with water from the Rio Grande, brought a bucket to be held in reserve. Gunn dug a small pit using a shovel he found in the wagon. He and Debbie helped her groaning father out of the wagon, led him to a spot near the pit, now filled with brush, cow and buffalo chips. Gunn struck a sulphur match, got the fire blazing. The heat was intense. Gunn set the larger pot directly on the flames, watched them lick up the sides, leave blackened streaks on the bottom.

"Get some rags, towels," he told the girl, "and a wooden scraper if you have one."

"I have some spoons of wood."

"That'll do."

Caleb Barnes was in a bad way. The sun was doing him no good. The man couldn't sweat properly. His breathing got worse. He looked, Gunn thought, like some imaginary creature one might see in picture books. At least he could walk, even though he was bowlegged as a mariner. The man didn't have much meat on him, was now fluffy as a moulting goose.

He sat there, Barnes did, rocking and groaning. Only his face, nose, eyes, mouth, showed that he was human. His eyes watered and Gunn could not tell their color. Red, at the moment.

"You're a mess," Gunn said, "but if you can bear the pain I'll scrape that stuff off of you."

"Leave me enough skin, I reckon I can grow most of it back."

"Don't talk, Pa," Debbie chided. "Save your strength." She didn't pronounce the "g" in the final word. Gunn couldn't pin down her accent though, or her father's. Western, probably. For a generation at least. The country was hard on folks, but those who survived became their own people with their own raw history.

The water boiled. Gunn let it get scalding hot, then grabbed a stick, draped a towel on it. He dipped the towel in the bubbling water.

"Lie down on your belly, Barnes. We'll try the back first, let you get used to the pain."

Debbie helped her father lie flat on his stomach.

Gunn ferried the dripping hot towel over to Barnes, dropped it just below his neck. The man screamed. His body quivered. Quickly, Gunn opened up the towel, whistling as the steaming cloth burned his hands. He pressed on it, then reached for the wooden spoon. He moved the towel down, began scraping oñ the tar. The back of the neck was fairly easy. The top of the back, too. Once he got started, the tar came off in slippery chunks. But there was a lot of it. The skin was raw where the tar had burned into the pores, blistered by the heat. Gunn winced, knowing that the worst was yet to come.

"You keep the towel hot, Debbie," Gunn said, "unless you want to scrape."

"No! I couldn't bear hurting him anymore."

Gunn tried to work fast. The towel didn't melt the tar, only made it more malleable. The water helped too. It worked its way under the caked-on tar and helped to loosen it. A lot of skin came off with the tar and feathers, but that couldn't be helped. And, the work was slow.

As they worked, Gunn asked Debbie questions. She seemed grateful for the distraction of conversation.

She told him that her pa had been pistolwhipped first. Gunn saw the marks on his scalp, the side of his face. He was saving that part for last. She said that Caleb had been a newspaperman for years and

13

finally had given up when his employers continued to neglect paying him on time. Sometimes they didn't pay him at all. He had become discouraged, wound up broke, working for a woman who owned a gambling hall in Socorro.

"I didn't stop there," Gunn told her. "A hunch, I guess. Some of those little trail towns can be mighty mean."

"This one is meaner than most," she said. "According to Pa. He never would let me go in the saloon, but I used to cry when he'd come home so tired he couldn't pull off his own boots."

"Go on, tell me what happened back there."

Debbie bowed her head, standing there with the stick in her hand, waiting for Gunn to give her back the towel. She looked ashamed, he thought. She hadn't tried to fix her dress and part of her breast still showed. Whatever had happened, he thought, she had been in it too.

"Pa, he—he always played cards for fun when he was writing for the journals. Then, at Lorna's place, Lorna Starr's the gal who owns the Rio Queen in Socorro, he started gambling for a living. She—that woman—encouraged him. He got really good. Too good. He started making a lot of money—a lot more than he ever did writing for newspapers—and I guess some people got jealous."

"What do you mean? Gambling's always been part of the West, these little clapboard towns."

"It's Nat Larrabee. He owns the Hog and Keg. He doesn't like competition much, I guess. According to what Pa told me."

Pa had passed out after Gunn started working on

14

his chest. The legs were still caked with tar and feathers, the face. Debbie winced when she saw the raw skin come off. She turned her head away, continued to talk.

"Lorna probably has the better place. They call her the Queen of Socorro. I saw her a time or two. A very beautiful woman, but hard. I don't know. Pretty, but like she's made of stone underneath. Do you know what I mean?"

"I reckon. Go on."

"Larrabee, he's been trying to drive her out, break her at the tables. Pa said he hired a bunch of professional gamblers, staked them, and sent them to the Rio Queen to play. Pa, he beat 'em. Every one. Larrabee's place has a nickname or a motto, you might say."

"What's that?"

"Whole hog or none."

"I heard of that place, then. Not Larrabee, but his place. Runs a couple of crooked games, I hear."

"Oh yes. Monte, faro, poker, the wheel. That's why he wants to ruin Lorna, so he can have it all. Anyway, after that night, Pa was warned to get out of town. I didn't know about it right then. He didn't say anything, didn't leave. Then this morning these men came to the house just before dawn. We were sound asleep. They dragged Pa out, started pistol-whipping him. They all had flour sacks with holes cut out for eyes, but I know they was Larrabee's men. When I screamed and tried to help, they knocked me around, ripped my dress. They loaded up all our things in the wagon and run us out of town early this morning. I was scared. I knew we couldn't

15

go back."

"Why? What did they say?"

"They—they said they'd kill my pa—and—and . . ."

She didn't need to finish. He saw it on her face. In her eyes.

Gunn's jaw went hard. A muscle quivered in his cheek. He knew about such men. They were no-account, boils on the flesh of the land.

He looked down at Caleb Barnes.

"Get me a real hot towel," he said tightly. "I'm going to get his face next. He got most of it on his legs and he's going to lose a lot of skin down there."

"Is he—will he—live?"

Gunn looked at her square.

"I don't know," he said. "Truly, I don't know."

CHAPTER TWO

Caleb Barnes stirred, but his breathing was shallow, weak.

Gunn worked very slowly around the face and neck. The tar had been slapped on just above the eyes and clear up to his chin. He wondered how Barnes had managed to breathe. He must have had thirty pounds of tar on his chest and back. His crotch would be difficult to work on too. The legs were coated thickly with both feathers and tar.

"Where were you going?" Gunn asked Debbie, after she was satisfied with the neck and face of the gambler.

"No place. Any place. But we can't leave. Everything we own is back there. Those men just threw in a bunch of things in the wagon. Our money is there, our friends. It's the first real home we ever had. Miss Starr treated us well, paid Pa handsomely."

Gunn looked at her with sympathy.

"You moved around a lot, I reckon."

"Every gold town or boom town. First thing in every new town is the newspaper. Pa worked for a man who was all promise. There were times when we didn't have food. He'd send a letter out by post, asking for his pay, but we'd always have to wait for a bank draft. He wrote for the Eastern magazines, too. It was the same. He wrote for *Harper's, Barron's,* several of the weeklies. They all used his stories and articles, but they didn't care much about paying him a decent wage."

"Mails are slow out this far."

"Years of it, Gunn. My pa wrote a lot and they always asked for more."

"Mighty impressive. So he went from writer to gambler."

"He said it was the same thing, only the money came faster at cards."

Gunn looked at the raw-skinned man with sympathy, if not downright pity. The man's color was not good. He didn't want to say anything to Debbie, but he'd seen few men in worse shape. Four or five hours of wearing tar wasn't good on a man. Barnes was bleeding in several places. He needed medical attention. Herbs, salve, an ointment, something to start healing him up. The bleeding was not profuse, just a general oozing through tiny pores where the skin had come off with the tar. But his general condition was not good.

"We get finished here, you'd better think about something to eat for your pa," Gunn said. "Those jaspers leave you any food? Something for a broth. And, we'd better pack him in mud, maybe mix some cow dung in with it."

Debbie reacted with a look of distaste.

Gunn shrugged. He'd seen it work on gunshot wounds. Indians mixing buffalo dung with clay, sealing off a wound. He was no medicine man, but Caleb Barnes was dying, would die, if he didn't start healing right up. No telling how bad he was hurt inside. Now that most of the tar was off, Gunn could see the bruises on his shoulders, ribs. Where he'd been pistolwhipped. He touched a spot on Caleb's ribcage. Likely a couple of ribs broken. He could wrap it and see if that helped. Broken ribs took a long time to heal, but if they were kept bandaged, the pain wasn't so bad.

The tar finally began to give on Caleb's legs. Luckily, the man had been in the wagon, out of the sun. Another day and . . .

"How is he?" Debbie asked, coming from the wagon. She had some dried beef jerky, an onion, some dried beans, a couple of potatoes in her hand.

"Hard to tell. Some stew might help. I think he's in shock. We need to get him in some shade. Under the wagon. Maybe we can rig a tent with that tarp."

"We're staying here?"

"Have to. Your pa can't be moved. He's got a couple of busted ribs, maybe some wounds inside him we can't see."

Debbie's face darkened. Her eyes widened with fear. Gunn turned away, pulled off the last of the big chunks of tar sticking to Caleb's ankle.

"I—I'll get Pa some clothes," she said, noticing that her father's genitals were exposed.

"No! We'll take those big pots and mix up some mud. He's going to hurt awful bad for a while."

Gunn hoped he was convincing enough. He had to hold out some hope to Debbie. Looking again at Caleb's face, though, he wasn't sure anything could help the man. He was one big raw wound, from toe-tip to topknot.

Debbie set up blankets under the wagon. Gunn rubbed mud all over Caleb's body, wrapped him loosely in a sheet. When the gambler came to, he was delerious, raving.

"He's in a lot of pain," Gunn observed. "The shade ought to help bring the fever down some. He really needs a *medico.*"

"All our money is back in Socorro. There's a doctor there too."

"Right now the trip might kill him. Best to lay over tonight, see how your pa is in the morning. You need some help fixing that grub?"

They had eaten hardtack and jerky for lunch, out of Gunn's saddlebags. Caleb had kept them busy most of the morning and part of the afternoon.

"No. Those men didn't give us much, but I can make a stew out of these vegetables and jerky. The wagon's a mess. I won't know what we have there until I go through it, straighten it out."

"I'll see if I can scare up a rabbit."

Gunn rode Duke back up the Rio Grande, scouting the country, the trail. He wanted to see, first of all, if anyone had followed the wagon. Some people were like buzzards. Scavangers. They'd follow a man in trouble, pick him clean. Gunn saw no sign of travelers or trackers. Satisfied, he made a wide circle, looking for game, a place to hole up, if they had to, for a few days. The country was wild, deserted. The white sands were blinding in the after-noon sun and he didn't want to cross the Rio if he didn't have to anyway. West, were mountains, timber. He rode into the foothills, jumped a jack rabbit, knocked it end over end with the .45. A clean shot. He had a brand new Winchester in his saddle boot, a gift from a gunsmith he had helped up in Tres Piedras a while back. The man had offered him a new Sharps, but it was not his idea of an all purpose saddle gun. All right for big game, buffalo, elk, moose, but not a weapon he wanted to pack around for fast work. Gunn dressed the rabbit out with his engraved knife, also a gift from a Mexican he had helped once.

The horse, Duke, though, was a special gift. From the Chinese girl, Soo Li. He was grateful to Ethan Morgan for the Winchester .44-.40, and to his daughter, Eva, for other things—but Soo Li would always have a special place in his heart. She had asked for nothing, given of herself willingly. He hoped she wouldn't meet a man who would make a door mat out of her. If she loved deep, she would give up her own freedom for the man who returned that love, or took it.

He arrived back at the wagon as the sun was throwing long saguaro shadows across the red earth. He smelled the aromas of cooking and his stomach tightened a notch. The rabbit was wrapped in its wet skin and he presented it to Debbie.

"In case you need it for your stew," he said.

She was delighted.

"Perfect. I can save the tinned beef until Pa feels a mite better. He did eat some broth though and I found a tad of whiskey in the tool box. He must have left it there a long time ago. Would it be all right to give him some tonight? He's hurting some-

21

thing fierce."

"Might have to, if he can't sleep. Is he bleeding any more?"

"No. I wet down the mud on his body. That seemed to help."

Gunn looked over at Caleb Barnes. The man was staring at Gunn. He lifted a hand, gesturing for Gunn to come over. Debbie didn't see the move. She was busy with the rabbit. The oxen had been unhitched, hobbled and were grazing nearby, chewing noisily on the sparse grasses. They eyed Gunn warily as he made his way to the wagon. They moved as if afraid they were going to be hitched up to the Conestoga again.

Gunn crawled under the wagon, into the shade.

It was hard looking into the eyes of the man he had recently de-feathered. The red-rimmed irises seemed to add to the haunting look of the pupils.

"Your name Gunn?" Caleb's voice was a low croak in his throat.

"I am."

"Heard of you. Good things, bad things."

"I reckon."

"Look at me, Gunn. You can face it, can't you? A man dying."

Gunn looked at him, winced inside.

"What is it, Barnes?"

"That girl out there. Debbie. She's all I have. Had. I'm not going to make it, son. I know that. I think I'm bleeding inside. I wrote an article for *Harper's* once about a fight I witnessed out in California. One of the fighters had his insides pounded to jelly. Wasn't a damn thing the doctor could do for him.

He bled to death, strangled on his own blood."

"That doesn't mean anything."

"I can feel it. Hear my lungs wheezing? One of those sonsabitches kicked me in the solar plexus, right under the ribcage. He knew what he was doing."

"Jesus, Barnes. You talk like a doctor. Or a fool. You can probably make it if the fever goes down."

Barnes stifled a cough, glanced at his daughter to see if she had noticed. Gunn saw that the man's complexion was bluish. Especially his lips. They had a pearly cast to them and now Gunn could hear the breath in Barnes' lungs. It sounded bad.

"You don't owe me any favors, Gunn. I know that. But I'm asking you to take care of my daughter. Get her away from Socorro. Away from Larrabee and his bunch. But I want you to go back on your own and see Lorna Starr. She—she's holding a lot of money for me. I want Deborah to have it."

"Likely, you'll be able to go back yourself someday. From what I hear, Larrabee's looking to buy himself a piece of ground six feet long and a pair wide."

"Don't count on it, Gunn. Larrabee's smart. And mean as a sidewinder. He lost a lot of money at my tables and he kicked shit out of me to get it back. He knows Lo—Miss Starr's holding it for me."

"You got a percentage?"

Caleb nodded, then turned purple as he stifled another coughing fit. Gunn watched him as the spasm passed.

"You'd better cough out some of that liquid in your lungs, Barnes. Or you'll get p-newmonia."

"Pneumonia, yes. That would be a blessing."

Gunn detected the education in the man's speech. The underlying intelligence that he had apparently neglected of late. Gamblers came from all parts of the country, from every kind of background. If a man had the fever, it didn't make any difference what schools he had attended, what life's pursuit he followed. The gambling fever had taken many a man and broken him on the wheel. Yet Barnes did not appear to have been broken. Rather, he had survived. Until now.

"You rest easy, Barnes." Gunn started to go. Barnes coughed, his eyes bleared.

"No, wait," he croaked. "There's something else. A journal. I kept a journal and Larrabee knows about it. He wanted me out of the way so he could look for it in our house."

"Is he apt to find it?"

Barnes nodded solemnly.

"And, if he does?"

"He'll come looking for me. He'll shoot me without a qualm."

"What's in the journal, Barnes?"

A coughing fit consumed the dying man. He spluttered and wheezed, fought for breath. His face turned a pale blue. Debbie, alarmed, ran over, knelt beside her father. Barnes struggled to speak, but the phlegm strangled him. He doubled over, fighting for breath.

"Leave him be," said Debbie. She turned her father over on his side so that he could expel the mucous in his throat. He hawked up a gob of phlegm, gasped and sank down on his stomach. Gunn stood up, found a canteen of water in the

24

wagon. He handed it to Debbie. She didn't acknowl-
edge it, but held it in her hands as she watched the
color suffuse her father's neck, the side of his face.

The man was obviously too weak to speak anymore. Gunn wandered back to the fire, threw some
wood on it.

There had been blood in the phlegm.

Caleb Barnes was a dying man. Larrabee wouldn't
have to come looking for him to finish him off.

Debbie was giving her father a drink of whiskey,
the water. That seemed to calm him.

Gunn stirred the stew, vaguely conscious that he
was hungry.

He wondered what was in the journal that could
be damaging to Larrabee. There was little law along
the Santa Fe trail. In Socorro it was probably a
token sheriff, a cubbyhole of a jail. Men like
Larrabee made the law. Made it work for themselves. There were a lot of questions he wanted to ask
Caleb Barnes, but now was not the time. If he lived
through the night . . .

He and Debbie ate silently while Barnes slept
under the wagon. She had rigged a sunshade from a
spare tarp and they sat under the shade listening to
her father's labored breathing. The waters of the Rio
Grande rippled by, gurgling in the eddies, whisper-
ing against the banks. A buzzard circled in the sky.
Both of them tried to ignore the scavenging bird.

Gunn dozed as Debbie cleaned up the plates and
pans, scrubbing them with sand, rinsing them in the
river. He was full, hot, even in the shade. Barnes
began mumbling in his sleep. Gunn couldn't understand a word. The afternoon droned on, dwindled to

a hushed twilight. Barnes didn't wake up, but he was still breathing.

"Sleep's the best thing for him right now," Gunn told her. Neither wanted any supper, but had eaten to keep their strength up. Debbie made some coffee that tasted of mud and brine. Gunn rolled a smoke, felt it scratch at his throat, burn his lungs.

"You want to ride on, don't you?" Debbie asked him pointblank as the first stars began to sparkle in the pale blue sky.

"Not in particular. I'll see you back to Socorro when your pa's better."

"He's not going to get better, Gunn. You know that and I know that."

Gunn was silent.

Debbie wept softly, then dried her eyes. Sniffled. Gunn felt sorry for her.

"I saw the blood. He's broken inside, Gunn. Before they tarred and feathered him, they beat him. Viciously. I—I never saw such cruelty before. He—he's going to die."

"You don't know that," he said lamely.

She fixed him with an accusing stare.

"I know my pa. I know what they did to him. He—he's not a strong man. Not anymore. All he has is his mind. That's always been strong. But his body, it's not strong."

He knew she was right. But it was not a good thing to talk about now. She was on the edge of hysteria. Close to screaming. Close to breaking down herself. He didn't know if he could handle it. Probably not. A dying man and a daughter going into hysteria was about the worst thing he could think of just now.

"Your pa mentioned a journal," Gunn said. "Know anything about it?"

Debbie snapped to a rigid position as if he had slapped her.

"Did he tell you about that?" Her voice was low, barely audible. A shade above a whisper. "My God, he must be dying." She paused, looked deep into Gunn's eyes. He sucked in a breath, waiting for her to continue. "Yes," she said, "he's been keeping a journal. I don't know what's in it. He always keeps a journal, though. A habit, I guess, from the years he spent writing. Breaking his heart." The sobs in her voice wrenched at Gunn's heart. "Yes, a journal. But this one is very important to him. More important than anything he's ever done, I think."

"What's in the journal?"

Debbie shook her head slowly.

"I—I don't know for sure. But it concerns Larrabee, and something he found out about him and the Hog and Keg. I'm certain sure of that."

"Gambling?"

"More than that."

"Cheating?"

"Oh, more than that, too. Something awful, I imagine."

"What was your pa going to do with the journal?"

"Write a story. A book. I don't know. Gunn, I don't care about that darned old journal. Just Pa. He—he's dying."

As if to emphasize her point, Caleb Barnes groaned, rose out of sleep, out of nightmare. His cry grated against nerve ends, galvanizing them into raw shock.

27

Debbie scrambled to her father's side, called out to Gunn a few moments later.

"Help me get him into the wagon. He—he'll be comfortable there."

Gunn lifted the man a few moments later, surprised at his lightness now that he was awake. Debbie got up in the wagon, helped pull him inside. Gunn left while she made her father comfortable. He heard them talking as he rolled a cigarette, lit it. He put out the fire, looked up at the far stars, the cold sliver of moon.

A pack of coyotes yapped across the river, their melodious cries floating over the land like ribbons of laughter. Starlight shimmered on the river waters and the fingernail of the moon danced like nervous mercury on the flowing surface.

Something else, as well.

Hoofbeats!

Gunn's senses shrieked. He ran to the wagon. Debbie was just climbing out the back. He grabbed her, clamped a hand over her mouth. She struggled, kicking and flailing her arms.

"Shut up!" Gunn whispered into her ear. "Someone's on the trail!"

He wrestled her to the ground, trying to be as gentle as he could, under the circumstances.

The hoofbeats got louder.

Debbie trembled. He threw an arm around her shoulder as they both lay peering into the darkness, the river at their backs. The hoofbeats slowed. They heard men's voices clearly in the still air. The words were indistinct.

Gunn looked back at the wagon, drew his pistol silently.

The wagon blended into the landscape, could not be seen unless the riders came right up to it. The top of its canvas skin looked like a low rise in the earth from the road, he knew. The night helped.

The riders stopped. Two hundred yards away.

"Hell, Gus, that wagon is long gone. We've been riding nigh on to two hours and no sign of it ner a fire."

"That fuckin' Nat! Sendin' us off on a wild goose chase. It's darker'n a mine pit out here."

Gunn saw a match flare. Faces bobbed ghostly above dark shapes. The match went out. Twin glows appeared, orange pinpoints.

"Let's ride back, Jake. Tell him they got clean away."

A pause.

"Reckon they did at that. Hell, they could have struck out for Roswell or gone south to Las Cruces or El Paso."

"Damn right."

"Wait up. That damned Hadnot's still back there. Hell, he thinks he can see in the dark."

"Mebbe he can."

Gunn couldn't hear what else was said. Instead, he tensed, as another rider joined the first two. There was a lot of low talk, and then, one of them said, in a loud voice: "Hell, I say we vote on it."

"No!" said another. "By God, I ain't ridin' with a man who sniffs the wind like a damned dog!"

"Shut up, Jake!"

29

One of the shadowed silhouettes separated from the bunch, went back up the trail. From the gait of the horse, a pony, Gunn figured it for the man who had ridden up last.

"Jesus, Jake, you hadn't ought to get personal."

"Fuck him, Gus. He ought to be put in his place."

There was more argument, but Gunn couldn't tell what it was about. The men tossed their cigarette butts into the air, wheeled their horses and rode toward Socorro, following the other rider, apparently.

Gunn let his breath out, waited a long time before he spoke. Hoofbeats faded into the distance.

"Know who they were?" Gunn whispered to Debbie. She was still trembling. She scooted sideways, was in his arms.

"Gus Whitcomb and Jake Early. Two of Larrabee's men. Gunmen. I—I'm scared to death. They were after us. Why? Haven't they done enough?"

Gunn held the shivering woman in his arms. She smelled of earth and sage. Smelled of fear.

"Who was the third man?" Gunn asked.

"I—I'm not sure."

"They called him Hadnot. Mighty peculiar name."

"There's a half-breed in town they call that. It could be him."

"Part Apache?"

"I—I think so. Why?"

"It might be important." Gunn didn't like it. Hadnot, or whoever he was, had wanted to go on, keep tracking. He was a loner. He had seen something back there, or smelled something. That crack one of them made about sniffing the wind

30

bothered him. An Apache could smell a man. Literally. Gunn said nothing to Debbie, but he resolved to stay alert.

"I reckon Larrabee didn't find that journal," he said quietly. "It must be damned important."

"Hold me, Gunn. Hold me tight. I can't stop shaking."

Gunn felt her breasts flatten against his chest.

Desire, unbidden, stirred in his loins. He held her tight, felt her shivers gradually subside.

When her face brushed against his, moments later, he tasted the salt of her tears. He pushed his pistol back in its holster. Boldly, he grasped her chin, tilted her face up to his. He kissed her hard on the lips, wondering if she would slap him for taking this liberty.

Debbie returned the kiss eagerly.

Her tongue slid past his lips, inside his mouth.

Gunn's manhood strained against the confinements of buckskin.

"I—I'll make us a bed," she husked.

"Yeah," Gunn growled low in his throat. "You better. This ground is getting awful damned hard."

CHAPTER THREE

He watched her shuck out of her dress. Faint light
rimmed her flesh, outlined the soft contours of her
body. Her dark hair seemed shot with silver, the
curls feathered tufts jutting out from the mass. Her
breasts uptilted, the nipples hard, plainly visible
against the shimmering waters of the Rio Grande.
She stood there as he slipped off his boots, shed his
buckskins.

Naked, he lay back in shadow.

"Do you want me, Gunn?" Her voice was
threaded with a different kind of fear. A quaver of
hesitation in it.

"Come down here," he husked, stretching out his
arms.

Her silhouette disappeared. Soft flesh touched his
hands. He drew her to him on the bedroll. Their
mouths touched. Her leg rubbed against the hard
stalk rising out of his groin. A breast grazed his
chest, soft, yielding.

A chill rose in the air, spun off the river by a faint
breeze. Neither of them felt the cool as they locked

together in an eager embrace. Debbie wallowed atop Gunn, smothering his face with kisses. She was like a swarm of bees about his neck, his ears. Her thatched crotch slid across his swollen cock, held there, quivering like some hungering creature come upon nourishment. He pushed upward, felt his organ press against the puffed lips of her sex.

Debbie felt his hardness, the visible proof of his desire for her.

She collapsed on him, her body quivering.

He held her close, caressed her face with kisses.

They rolled and tossed in the shadowy night world of saguaros and faint stars. The oxen lowed nearby and Duke, scenting the mating of humans, snorted.

Gunn's hand grasped a breast, kneaded it gently. Teased the rubbery nipple with the flat of his thumb. She let out a soft, mewling sound and presented his hand with the other breast. He gave it equal attention, tantalizing the nipple until it hardened like a tiny thumb. He kissed both nipples, felt her body quiver.

His hand found the thatched mound between her legs.

Pried her legs apart, groped the sex-cleft deftly with probing fingers. She was wet, the silken inner lining of her labials oozing a steamy honey. He slid his finger up and down, felt her body tauten with desire.

"Yes, Gunn," she breathed. "I—I knew it would be like this. I knew it would be right and that you would be gentle with me."

"You know a great deal," he acknowledged.

"I—I kept watching your eyes. And Pa trusts you. He is a good judge of men. Of character."

"He likely wouldn't think much of my character right now if he knew . . ."

A finger pressed against his lips.

"Hush. It's bad enough knowing he's up there, hurt, in pain . . ."

Gunn's finger slipped inside her, encountered the heat, the damp pudding of her, pulsating with desire. She wriggled, sighed, and kissed him hard on the mouth where her finger had pressed him to silence.

"Now," she gasped. "I—I can't wait any longer."

She rolled off his frame, onto her back. Her hand reached out for him, grasped the swollen staff. Squeezed it. He felt ice and fire race up his spine. The ground spun in a sudden rush of giddiness. His stalk throbbed with the lusting beat of blood.

Debbie slid her legs wide to receive him. She released her hold on his manhood.

He pulled himself up above her, looked down at her shadowy face. He could not see her eyes, only their dark hollows. Her breasts jutted up from her chest like dark melons dusted with silver. He hovered over her form, the delicately rounded tummy, the gaunt lean thighs, the wide-spread legs. He hovered there, drinking in her elusive beauty, her sensuous body basking in saguaro shadows. Hers was the beauty of youth and eagerness, of unleashed desire and womanly hunger.

He felt her eyes staring up at him. She opened her mouth, licked her lips with the tip of her tongue.

For a moment, he thought he was in another place, another time.

With Laurie.

But Laurie was dead.

Still, he remembered the woman had been his wife, his life. Remembered her naked and willing beneath him. Remembered her soft laugh, her sweet scents.

Debbie waited for Gunn to enter her.

He hung there on the edge of memory, blinking his eyes as if to assure himself that he was not back in Colorado, on the Poudre, with Laurie.

"Gunn? Is something wrong?"

He shook his head.

"No."

He dipped down, his cock plunging into her waiting sheath. Sank effortlessly through lubricated labials into the steaming cauldron of her sex. She winced, squirmed, as he skewered her. Her hips shimmied as he bored deep, sliding smoothly into her.

Her hands found his back. The fingernails dug in.

"Ooooh!" Debbie cried, as her body bucked with the first quick orgasm.

Gunn sank to the base of his root, hung there while her quivering passed through his own flesh.

She cried out again and fingernails sliced into his back.

She gasped, breathlessly.

"It was so quick," she sighed. "So beautiful."

Debbie was not a virgin and Gunn was glad.

35

She had been up the road before. It made things simpler, especially under the circumstances. An ailing father, her life in some danger, she needed all the simplicity she could get at such a time. He didn't want to be the first with Debbie. He sensed that she was going to come to more grief and he didn't want her to be dependent on him. That had happened to him more than once.

She relaxed after that first climax. Her fingers began to massage his back instead of trying to peel him like an orange. Her hips began to match his rhythms, flowing with him as he plumbed her depths. He stroked her slow, then fast, felt her breath quicken as she surged toward still another climax. Inside, she was wet and hot. Very hot. Her sex-cleft squeezed his cock as she used muscles adroitly. Yes, she had been up the road. She was very good.

"Do you like me, Gunn?"

"Yes."

"I want to please you."

"You do."

He sank deep and she exploded in a sudden orgasmic shudder.

The wildcat in her returned. Fingernails raked his bare back. Her hips thrashed savagely. She cried out, bucked against him with a fury that snatched his own breath away.

He kissed her hungrily and she scraped teeth across his lip.

Her breasts seemed to swell against his chest. He felt the quivering in her pelvis, the heat from her loins. Her tongue slithered into his mouth and he felt a stab of sensation rise from his groin.

Again and again she bucked with orgasm.

At times, Gunn felt as if he was holding on for dear life. She rammed her pelvis up high and he sank still deeper, probing the mouth of her womb. She thrashed, roiling the bedclothes into a swirling mass. Her legs lifted up and encircled his hips. She rocked with him through several smaller, electric orgasms, then screamed as a thundering jolt of pleasure surged through her body. She bit him on the shoulder, dug in her fingernails as she rode it out, sobbing mindlessly, tearlessly.

"Give it to me, Gunn. All of it! Oh, it's so good, man . . . so damned good!"

He was amazed at her energy, the power of her orgasms. The more he gave her, the more she wanted. It was a wild ride, like going to hell in a hand-car, straight down, faster and faster, each orgasm wilder than the last. His back he knew, must be cut to ribbons, but he felt no pain. Only the swelling sea of her body beneath him, the choppy waves of energy lashing at him like wind. He pinned her down, bored into her, pushed up to scrape across the hard point of the button inside her.

"Oh, you know how to do it!" she exclaimed. "You're touching it. You're driving me mad."

He lasted longer than he thought he would. Or thought he could.

He felt her energy wane, speeded up his strokes.

Debbie writhed as if consumed by an inner fire.

"Now," she breathed. "Come now. Spill your

37

spunk in me."

Her words were a lash to his passion.

Gunn's blood raced. He finished up in a lathering burst of speed. Debbie cried out in exultation as her own passion-flames were fanned by Gunn's short quick strokes. She bucked and thrashed beneath him.

Gunn stopped, shuddered, as his seed burst from its sac, spewed into the deep cone of her sex.

He felt the sharp pain of her fingernails knifing through his back.

A wave of sweet lassitude washed over him. He fell atop her, cushioned by her loins, her breasts. Her screams rang in his ears. In the cool, his body glistened, slick with sweat. Debbie too, was damp with perspiration. He smelled the earth and the wind in her hair. He kissed her in gratitude, conscious that his lower lip was sore from her biting. There would be a mark on his shoulder as well as scratches on his back. Love wounds. Reminders that he had lain with a woman. A good woman.

"It was wonderful," she said later. "Beautiful."

"Yes," said Gunn quietly, rolling over on his back. He stared up at the stars. They seemed brighter, more brilliant than light-shot diamonds. As always, he felt renewed, whole. The woman beside him was important, as they all were. Her scents lingered in his nostrils, like invisible wisps of memory. The actual moment of climax was forgotten, too brief to capture, yet the essence of the woman remained. The tigress in her, the kitten. The savage, the tamed.

"I'm not sleepy," she said. "I ought to be, but

I'm not."

"I know. Neither am I."

"I wish we could stay like this forever."

The moments stretched out, but flew away nevertheless. Moments without moorings. They both wanted to stop time and time wouldn't stop. Gunn closed his eyes, shutting out the stars. Debbie moved against him and he felt the softness of her breast brushing his ribs.

"I wish I had known you before," she said. "First."

"It's not important."

"Yes." A bitterness there that he could feel, hear. Jarring.

"Why?"

"The first time wasn't good. Wasn't like this. I wanted it to be, but I was too scared, the boy too rough, too inexperienced."

"Did you . . . ?"

"Love him? No. I thought I did. I wanted him. I wanted someone. It was a mistake. Pa found out and made it worse. He thought I should be pure, wrapped in crinoline with ribbons tied in my curls. Forever. I hated Pa for that, but then I understood."

"That's good. We don't always understand what happens to us when we're young."

"I think you did. I think you always understood."

"No."

"Your eyes. I can see them now. Even in the dark. They're so wise. Sometimes they're like smoke and at others, like a pale blue sky. I guess they're gray, or blue. I've never seen eyes like them. I think that's why I wanted you. Tonight. Even if tomorrow is a

39

terrible day, I wanted tonight. With you."

Her hand found him, hefted the limp muscle.

Gunn kept his eyes closed. The tiredness was there, just on the edge. But her hand was warm and the night cool. The sweat was drying on his body, icing him over. But he felt strong.

"My," she marveled, "it doesn't take much for you, does it?"

He had no answer for her. But he began to swell again and Debbie leaned over, kissed him in that yearning savage way. Her tongue probing his mouth, touching off sparks in his loins.

He grabbed her, drew her to him. His blood thundered in his temples.

After a while, he took her again and she loved him with the wildness of a woman who knows there may be no tomorrow, who knows it may be for the last time. And the night closed over them, turned cold at midnight so that they had to burrow into their blankets and hold onto each other for warmth.

* * *

The unshod pony made no sound on the hard earth.

There was no rider in the saddle.

Instead, the man walked in front of the pinto, stopped now and then to peer at the road with intent eyes. Often, he stopped, put a hand to the earth as if feeling for a track. It was chilly and his breath plumed into the air every time he exhaled. The pony's twin nostrils blew forth heavy plumes as it followed the man obediently, silent as a painted ghost.

At one point, the man left the road, headed toward the river.

He paused, stood straight, sniffed the air.

The river scent overpowered all others.

The man was stocky, short, with powerful arms and shoulders, thick legs. He wore moccasins, dark trousers, a colorful shirt. A bright headband graced his wide forehead, held down his shock of jet-black hair. His high-crowned hat was black, sported a single eagle feather in its dark band.

The sky began to pale imperceptibly when he saw the wagon.

He tied the pinto to a saguaro, crept up to the rear of the wagon quiet as a cat.

He listened for a long time to the sounds of breathing from within.

Puzzled, he put his ear to the canvas.

One man, he thought. *All alone.*

He stepped away from the wagon, circled it. He stooped down, brushed the ground with sensitive fingers. He sniffed the air hard. The man inside the wagon groaned. The halfbreed stiffened, then walked away, hunched over, toward the river.

Willie Hadnot carried a rifle in one hand. On his belt was a knife, pistol.

He made no sound as he flitted from saguaro to saguaro, a shadow among shadows. The night sky began to pull away from the eastern horizon as the pale glow widened like a slit in a dark curtain.

He passed the oxen, just rising from their wallow.

Their hides were wet with dew, glistened in the light.

The horse eyed him and Willie froze until it lost interest in him.

He was not surprised to see the horse. He knew it would be there. Jake and Gus had not listened to him and there had been no use arguing with them. If they had continued on their way a while longer, looked at the tracks, they would have known that a rider had joined up with the wagon, left the road. At first it had been only a hunch, but now he knew. An hour's ride out of Socorro, Jake had broken out a bottle from his saddlebags. The two white men had started drinking. They had offered him a drink, but he had refused. Larrabee did not pay him to drink, but to track. And he was proud of that part of him that could do that.

Willie's mother was an Apache. His father, a trapper named Sam Hadnot. Sam had died five years ago of the fever and his mother had gone off to live with the remnants of her tribe in old Mexico. The white blood in him had kept him in New Mexico where he earned a living any way he could. Anything to keep from living the hard ways of his people, always on the run, ridden with disease and mites. Nat Larrabee paid him extra money for jobs like this one. And promised much more after he got rid of his competition.

But Willie didn't want to think of that now. He had his quarry. Somewhere. Near.

He crept down the slope toward the river, his senses keen, his blood racing with excitement.

Gus and Jake were probably still wondering

where he was. He had watched them drink at a friend's shack outside of town until they had all gotten drunk enough to ride on in and report to Larrabee. Or pass out. They would hate it like hell that he doubled back and found Barnes, but he didn't owe them anything. Larrabee would likely dress them down and forget about it. Or, he might say nothing at all. Larrabee was hard to figure.

Well, he had gotten out of that. They would be looking for him when they sobered up, but he might even be back in Socorro by then.

The sky began to lighten quickly, and the chill from the earth rose up almost like a wind birthing.

Willie did not shiver, but steeled himself for what he had to do.

A splash from the river startled the halfbreed. He peered down at the murky waters, saw them swirling with milky light. The splash was weak, as of a fish jumping lazily for a vagrant insect.

He moved away from the saguaro, saw the dark shape sprawled on the ground a few yards away.

He moved closer, careful to make no sound.

Two humps in the blankets. Closer still, padding on noiseless puma feet. A shadow in the morning light.

He wanted to make sure. The man who owned the dun had to be taken out first. He expected no trouble from the white woman.

The sun rose higher, kissed the horizon, just under the rim. Light hovered over the far hills. The sky turned peach, then flamed a raw orange.

Willie could see very clearly now, thirty yards

away from the blankets, the twin mounds.

The girl's face showed clearly. Her eyes were closed, her hair spread out like a fan.

Willie brought the rifle up. The vague sound of the river whish-sloshing against the shore was the only sound of the still morning. The halfbreed squeezed the trigger of the lever-action Winchester slightly, thumbed back the hammer. The cocking made only the faintest sound, inaudible a foot away. There was a round in the chamber. He brought the hammer back to full cock.

He put the butt to his shoulder, sighted down the barrel. There was now enough light to see clearly. He could not see the man's head, only his shape in the blankets. Next to the woman.

The river murmured against the banks as Will drew in a breath. Held it.

He brought the front sight down to the largest mass of the blanket. He would not try for a head shot. For the chest.

The sleeping woman did not stir.

The sun slipped up over the horizon, a boiling mass of flame.

The saguaros, the earth, lit up like a stage set.

Willie squeezed the trigger.

Smoke and flame belched from the end of the rifle barrel. A puff of dust rose up from the plucked blanket where the bullet slammed home.

Debbie rose up, screaming, her face a livid mask of horror.

Willie cocked the rifle quickly, rammed another live shell into the chamber.

He fired again.

The shot echoed across the country like the first as the blanket twitched with a fresh bullet hole.

"Gunn! You've killed him!" screamed Debbie.

Willie grinned wide, started toward her, lavering another shell into the chamber just in case.

CHAPTER FOUR

The lever's action clicked loudly in the awesome silence as another round slid into the barrel, cocking the rifle at the same time.

Debbie screamed.

"You killed him, you savage!"

"He was in the wrong place at the wrong time, lady." Willie's smirk of satisfaction was not lost on Debbie.

She glared at the halfbreed, her blue eyes glittering with hatred. She seemed afraid to look at the smoking heap next to her. She smelled gunpowder and burning wool. The mass of fire in the east was split by the horizon, half of it throwing a fiery orange ribbon across the Rio Grande. A saguaro shadow fell across her lap as she clutched her blanket to her naked breasts.

Willie heard the splash of water, the ominous metallic click of a cocking hammer.

His expression froze on his face, a mask of blank puzzlement.

Debbie's eyes swung to the riverbank.

Willie wheeled, raking the rifle along with his movement.

Gunn rose up from the water's edge, pistol in hand.

"Drop it!" he called to the halfbreed.

Willie hesitated, his dark eyes flickering. The distance between the two men was less than fifty yards. Their eyes met. Willie's finger moved on the trigger. He moved the rifle barrel in line with his target.

Gunn fired. A fleeting look of sadness swept across his eyes, like a gray shadow.

Willie squeezed the trigger of his rifle.

Particles of seconds separated the two explosions.

Debbie's scream sandwiched in between.

"No, don't kill him!"

Gunn wondered who she was screaming at because he heard her clearly and yet could not see her through the white pall of smoke. A split-second later, his skin crawled as the rifleman's bullet sizzled past his ear. He heard the bullet smack into the river, whine off in a ricochet.

Willie's scream overpowered Debbie's.

Gunn thought he could hear the sickening crunch of the bullet as it struck flesh and bone.

As the smoke cleared, he saw the halfbreed stagger. The rifle fell from his hands, clattered against a rock.

Debbie half-rose out of the blankets, flashing bare breasts, alabaster skin.

Gunn ran toward the wounded man, cocking his pistol in case he needed another shot.

47

Willie clawed at his back. His legs wobbled as he staggered in a circle. The bullet had slammed through his gut, nicked his spine. A slow paralysis numbed him. He vomited blood and bile, twisted as if to reach the site of the pain. His legs collapsed and he hit the ground. He continued to twist in a circle as if helpless to stop himself. He clawed at his knife, drew it, finally.

"What have you done to him?" Debbie gasped, the light of hysteria dancing in her blue eyes.

Gunn said nothing, but looked at the dying man.

Willie stopped moving, his legs kicking spasmodically. He brought the knife blade up to his neck, held the point near his jugular vein. He looked at Gunn through glazed eyes. Eyes of pain, of defeat.

"Shoot me dead," he said quietly.

"You're done for," said Gunn.

"I know it. Make it quick."

"No!" screamed Debbie. Her scream was a hoarse grating rasp that sent a shock up Gunn's spine. He did not look at her, but at the halfbreed, whose shirt was stained with bloody vomit. The stench was overpowering. It clung to the insides of his nostrils like verminous bats clinging to a cave wall. It was the stench of death, of ignominy.

Sweat broke out on the wounded man's face. Oozed out of the pores, bathed his dark skin with a slick oily sheen. Gunn knew he was in agony. An agony that few men could stand for very long. The way the man had behaved told him that the .45 caliber slug was probably lodged next to his spine. Shooting pain all through his body. His legs had gone out from under him, too, as if he had no control over them. It was a sickening thing to see a man die this way, to hurt so goddamned much at the end. Even if that man was an enemy.

An enemy he had not wanted, nor sought.

Gunn's thoughts drifted back to the predawn quiet. Moments before he had crawled out of the bedroll, uneasy, listening. A hunch. More than that. An instinct. A premonition that something was wrong. He had jolted awake for no reason, listened to the even sound of Debbie's breathing, the gurgle and flap-splash of the river sloshing the banks, the far-off yap of a coyote that cut off as if a knife had slashed across the animal's throat.

Dressing quietly in the dark, he had listened to the night sounds, trying to filter them out. But it wasn't any sound he had heard. Just a feeling and a sense that something was going to happen. He knew the source of the feeling, too, as he woke up, walked to the river, scouted a place to hide. The three riders. One of them had been a loner. That was what had bothered him. But he had buried it. And his sleep had brought it up to the surface again. That third rider, so close, yet drawn away by the other two. A lone wolf, though, for sure. And men like that always came back. This one had. A tracker. A half-breed.

Willie's lips took on a bluish cast. Spittle collected at the corners of his mouth. He held the knife close to his neck, the blade pointed at a spot just under his jaw, two inches under his ear lobe.

"Come on, shoot you bastard," hissed the half-breed.

"You came after me to kill me," Gunn said. "Why?"

"You know why."

"Maybe. Was it worth it, man?"

Debbie stood up, her face waxen.

Gunn glanced at her, saw that she was trembling in the morning chill. The sun gilded her flesh, made her look like a shining golden statue. The halfbreed looked at her too. Winced in pain. But, there was something else. A look between them. Gunn felt the shock of surprise, as if someone had just poured a bucket of cold water over his head.

A spasm passed through Willie Hadnot's body.

He continued to stare at Debbie, who was holding the blanket with one hand so that it covered only a small portion of her body. Her arms and thighs gleamed in the sunlight, her hair radiated.

Gunn saw the movement, leaped forward, his arm outstretched.

Too late!

Hadnot drew the sharp knife across his own jugular, cutting deep. Blood gushed from the wide slash.

Debbie sucked in a breath, gasped. Her eyes went wide in shock. As if the knife had cut her own throat.

Gunn grabbed Hadnot's wrist, but the damage was done. Blood pumped from the man's neck in crimson freshets. The glaze in the halfbreed's eyes thickened, turned frosty in the shadow of a saguaro. The man opened his mouth, but no sound came out. His lips worked like a fish's. Gunn snatched the knife away, instinctively, stood up in disgust.

Hadnot slid down on his back. The sun struck his eyes, but he did not blink. He stared straight up at the sky and his mouth closed as a convulsion ripped through him.

"Who was he?" Gunn asked Debbie.

"W—Willie Hadnot. Is he—he . . ."

"He's dead. Or almost."

Hadnot's chest moved slightly, but it was only a spasm. The blood from the gaping neck wound pooled up, soaked into the red earth. The man's sphincter muscle gave way and the stench rose up in the air. A mist drifted over from the shrouded river. Enveloped them in a hazy light that was rosy and gray. Gunn threw the knife down and holstered his pistol. He walked over to Debbie, took her in his arms.

She nestled her head in his chest and began sobbing uncontrollably. Gunn stood there, letting her ride out her hysteria. If that's what it was. She had known Willie, obviously, but had denied it the night before. Or had he imagined that? He tried to remember the conversation, but it wouldn't come. Did she know Hadnot? Or was it only death that frightened her? He couldn't be sure, but there was something wrong here. Something he couldn't pin down. He let it go.

"You'd better get some clothes on, see how your father is. The shots probably woke him up."

"Pa . . . !" Debbie seemed to snap back into herself. Her eyes came back into focus and she scrambled frantically for her clothes.

"I'll take care of things here," Gunn said, but he doubted if Debbie heard him. In a few moments, she was running up the hill toward the wagon. She stopped once, and looked back, but he waved her on. He didn't want her to see what he had to do.

The oxen began lowing as the earth came to life.

51

Gunn knew what he had to do. To leave a dead man out in the baking sun would be to invite cholera. The ground was too hard, too rocky, to consider burying the halfbreed. Piling rocks over him wouldn't help much either. Keep the coyotes and buzzards away from his carcass for a while, but the stench would hang in the air day and night until the worms and flies, ants and small rodents finished up the rotting flesh.

Quickly, Gunn stripped the corpse of its gunbelt, wallet, boots. No use letting anyone else paw over the dead man. He dragged Willie Hadnot's body to the Rio Grande, then picked him up by shirt collar and crotch. Counting to three and heaving mightily, Gunn tossed the body into the river. It landed with a splash, sank. The swirling waters caught it, twisted it around, bobbed the head back up into view. The head drifted slowly down river until it disappeared. Gunn walked back to the spot where the man had died, picked up his things and threw them in the center of the bedroll. He picked up the blankets and carried them up to the wagon.

Debbie had a cookfire going.

Caleb Barnes was awake, groaning in pain. Gunn looked inside the wagon after throwing the bedding down in a heap.

"Morning," he said quietly.

"I heard shooting. Debbie won't tell me what happened."

"Nothing much. We were jumped by a man called Willie Hadnot."

"That bastard," Caleb croaked.

"You knew him?"

Caleb went into a coughing fit. Gunn saw that the man's body was a mass of ugly scabs. Many of these were cracked and oozing.

"Trash," gasped Barnes. "Help me out of here, Gunn."

"You ought to stay put, out of the sun."

"I can't breathe in here."

Gunn helped the man out. He needed medical attention. His flesh was raw in those places that had not begun to scab. Blood and clear fluid seeped through the scabbed spots and most of the mudpack had dried and fallen off his body.

Caleb's eyes were red-rimmed, his features gaunt.

"Pa, be careful," said Debbie, her voice low, her face turned away from Gunn's deliberately.

What was wrong here?

Debbie got a sheet from the wagon, wrapped her father in it. Gunn helped her lean him against a wagon wheel. She put a feather-ticking pillow behind her father. He grimaced in pain and Gunn could hear the breath whistling through his bronchials. The man had water in his lungs. Likely he would get pneumonia before the day was out. It was not something he wanted to see, a man struggling for breath, drowning before his eyes. But, it might be a merciful death at that. He wondered if Debbie knew.

Later, after she had gotten some hot broth into her father's stomach, she spoke to Gunn alone, in whispers.

"What did you do with . . . ?" she asked.

"You don't want to know," he told her.

"Yes, I do."

"Buried him. In a way."

53

She winced, avoided his gaze.

"How?"

"Debbie, what was Hadnot to you?"

"Nothing," she said quickly. Too quickly. But, she dropped the subject and Gunn didn't press it.

They made a bed under the wagon for Caleb. He lay down, shivering, and Gunn hauled mud up from the river, packed it thick on his body. Caleb's breathing got worse.

"How long does he have?" Debbie asked him on one of his trips.

"A day or so. We could try and get him to a doc, but I don't think he'd last the trip."

"No. He sounds bad. He looks so small and frail." Debbie was trying hard not to cry.

"Don't give up hope," Gunn said quietly. But there was no weight to his words. Caleb Barnes was dying. The mud might help his wounds, but there was nothing either of them could do about the fluid building up in his lungs.

Debbie saw to the oxen, leading them to the river to drink, while Gunn took care of the horses, his own and the one that belonged to Hadnot. He stripped the pinto of saddle and bridle, hobbled it. The horses foraged along the riverbank for the sparse grasses, fought off flies through the heat of day. Toward afternoon, Caleb went into delerium, his fever raging. Debbie tried to cool him down with towels drenched in water, but the fever didn't break until just before night fall.

Gunn shot a rabbit for supper. Debbie boiled it to provide broth for her father. She heated beans from an airtight can and made coffee. She and Gunn ate sparingly, scarcely talking. Instead, they listened to the hard breathing coming from Caleb's blankets. Every time his breathing caught, Debbie jumped. Several times she seemed about to say something important to Gunn, but each time she clamped her mouth shut and remained silent. Still, as he rolled a smoke after supper, he realized that she was fighting an inner battle that somehow concerned him. It was not in his nature to press, however, so he strolled away from the campfire's dying embers and stood along the riverbank, listening to the soothing sounds of the flowing water. The smoke scratched at his throat and he tossed the cigarette into the water. The faint hiss as it landed was barely audible above the sound of the river lapping against the bank. The waters glistened with the reflections of starlight. Bats scooped insects out of the air on both sides, darting like black knives on silent wings.

Debbie appeared, a few moments later. She put her arm around Gunn's waist, clung to him.

"I need you," she said quietly.

"How's your pa?"

"I don't think we should put him inside the wagon tonight. He's sleeping and I don't want to wake him up."

"No. We can keep an eye on him better if he stays under the wagon."

"He spoke to me a while ago. About the manuscript. He told me where it was."

"Oh?"

"Under one of the boards in the house. In the kitchen, next to the stove."

"It seems pretty important to him."

55

"Socorro was important. He thought he could make a life there. He was wrong."

"It's not much of a town."

"He didn't like big towns. He always met heartbreak in them. He got to the point where he wanted to be alone more than he wanted to be with people. And even with people he just wanted to be one of them. He told me once that a writer never did quite fit in. He was always on the outside, observing, writing down the manners, the habits, the sins—and hiding his own from himself."

"Your pa's a pretty smart man."

"I think so. Broken as he is, I respect him. I love him too, but I don't think a man should go against his nature."

"What do you mean?"

He knew what she meant. He just wanted to hear her say it.

"Pa wasn't a gambler. It wasn't his nature. He was a man who loved life, and, especially, people. He saw the bad things, but he tried to balance them in his writing. When he gave that up, he lowered himself. Gambling brought him, us, to grief. I would think you could see that, Gunn. You've lived. You know how people are."

"I reckon."

The silence filled in around them. Debbie took her arm away from his waist and walked to the river. She stooped down, scooped up a handful of water. She dabbed her face, stood up, her face gleaming in the starlight.

She walked back to stand in front of Gunn. Looked up at him, her face bathed in shadow.

"You want to know about Willie Hadnot, don't you?" she asked bluntly.

Gunn sucked in a breath.

His senses tingled as if someone had drawn a feather's hard edge across the nape of his neck.

"Only if you want to tell me," he said.

"I—I do—and I don't. I'm wondering what you'll think of me."

"Why? It's what you think of yourself that counts."

"I don't think much of myself right now." She paused, and Gunn was silent. He could feel the struggling going on inside her. Could sense it as if some part of her mind was sentient, palpable, reaching out to touch him like the hand of a child. "Just promise me, Gunn, that you won't tell Pa. It would break his heart."

"You don't have to tell me anything, Debbie. Unless it's too heavy for you to tote by yourself."

Debbie breathed a sigh of relief. Her shoulders sagged as if she was shrugging off a great weight.

"I guess that's part of it. I've carried this around with me for weeks now and it's too late to change any of it. Sooner or later it was bound to come out, but I was hoping that he might . . . might . . ."

Her voice caught and Gunn thought she was going to cry. She needed to cry.

"It's about the Hadnot feller, isn't it?"

Debbie nodded.

"I had to kill him, Debbie. If I'd been sleeping in that blanket, I'd be dead now."

"I know that," she said quickly. "That's what makes it so hard. I hate killing. I hate death! Oh, damn damn damn!"

He waited, as her voice faded to a murmur.

"I hate it too," he said, finally. "Was Hadnot your beau?"

A far star, or a comet, tumbled through space. A trail of silver light arced across the heavens as if someone had struck a match on the black void of night.

"I'm carrying his child," said Debbie. "I'm going to have a breed for a baby."

CHAPTER FIVE

Caleb Barnes died before sunrise.

He called out to Debbie and she rose from the blankets to tend him. Gunn woke up too and lit a lantern. In the bobbing light, he looked at the gaunt face of the dying man and locked his teeth tight. The look in Caleb's eyes told him all he needed to know. The man looked at them and right through them. To a beyond only he could see. A frail hand reached out for his daughter's.

"Pray for me," he croaked.

"Pa . . ."

"Don't let Larrabee . . ."

Barnes coughed, then strangled. The lantern light danced on his sweat-drenched face. A face turning blue. Debbie screamed softly, grabbed her father by the shoulders. It was too late.

Caleb's throat rattled. His eyes rolled up in the back of their sockets. His lips pearled over with a blue cast. He shuddered and his eyes closed.

Debbie shook him, crying out to him.

Gunn touched her shoulder gently.

"He's gone, Debbie," he said.

The tears came then. Deep wracking sobs shook her body. He helped her lay her father flat on his back, then took her in his arms. He let her cry it all out and then pulled a sheet over her father's face as Debbie stumbled away to be alone with her grief.

Gunn found a spade inside the wagon's tool box. Debbie would never stand still for floating Caleb's body downstream. He found a soft spot on a hill, began clearing it of stones. He dug a shallow grave, sweating in the rising sun. It was hard work, but he got the hole down to a foot and a half in depth and figured it would take him another hour to go six more inches, two hours or more if he tried for another foot.

When he got back to the wagon, he saw that Debbie had bathed and dressed her father's body, combed his hair. Luckily, Caleb's eyes had remained shut in *rigor mortis*.

"There aren't any flowers," Debbie said.

"No, not this time of year."

"I'll come back in the spring."

"Yes." Gunn thought of all the graves he'd seen beside the trails. Especially in the Southwest. In Mexico. Some of them with flowers. In November, on All Souls' Day, the Mexican families made pilgrimages to those roadside graves and festooned them with bouquets, with flowers grown in the huts, the *jacales*. Some of the graves had crosses, some stones. It would not be like that for Caleb Barnes. Not today.

"I'll fetch a sheet," Debbie said. Her voice was dull, like lead, heavy. Gunn saw that she had washed her face, tied her hair up. She had found a bonnet in the wagon and tied that on her head. She wore a print dress that had faded, but was clean. She wore sandals on her feet. She did not cry when Gunn lifted the rigid body of her father up and carried him over to the depression on the small hill. She walked a little ahead, a determined lilt to her step, her chin held high. She clutched the sheet in her arms as if it was a child's garment, something precious.

Gunn laid her father in the grave, face up. He straightened the legs, pulled his arms down along his sides.

"Fold his hands across his middle," Debbie said, her voice stony as granite. "He slept that way sometimes."

Gunn had to work at it, but he fixed the hands to her satisfaction.

"I'll put the sheet over him," she said, bending down next to the grave. Gunn stepped back and watched her.

She spread the sheet out on one side of the grave, folded it double. She leaned over, kissed her father's cheek. She put her hand on one of his, squeezed. The seconds ticked by and Gunn thought she was never going to let go. Tears oozed out of her tight shut eyelids. He almost stepped forward and pulled her away, but he could see her lips moving in a silent prayer. It was a godawful moment. He felt wrenched inside, pulled apart by her grief.

Finally, Debbie released her grip on her father's hand and stood up. She put a hand on Gunn's arm and squeezed him gently. Then, she walked away, unable to look at the grave.

Gunn waited until she had gone back to the

wagon, then began shoveling dirt over the sheet-shrouded body of Caleb Barnes. He packed the mound down and covered the grave with stones. A hawk's shadow floated over the grave and Gunn looked up. The hawk wheeled and floated off toward the low hills, hunting with fierce eyes.

Debbie was packing the bedrolls in the wagon when Gunn returned with the shovel.

"You may just as well take Hadnot's knife and gun. You might want to give it to your child if it's a boy."

"N—no. I don't want any reminders of Willie."

"But . . ."

Debbie fixed him with a sharp look.

"It wasn't what I wanted. Willie took me, Gunn. Against my will. But no one would think that. I—I liked him at first, before I knew who he was, who he worked for. And maybe I made up to him a little too much. But I didn't want that. He took advantage of a kindness and violated me."

"I'm sorry. I didn't know . . . I figured . . ."

"I know what you figured and that's sad. Men have the advantage in this world and it makes me a little sick. Especially when I think of Pa lying in that grave over there, killed before his time by such men as think they can walk over anybody who gets in their way. I'm glad you killed Willie Hadnot. He would have raped me again if he was in your spot. I don't like killing, but I hated Willie. I hate him even more now because I feel like I pulled the trigger myself."

She didn't break down or cry as Gunn expected her to. Instead, she tossed the bedding inside the wagon and went off after the oxen. Gunn picked up Hadnot's weapons and threw them in the wagon. There was no comfort he could give Debbie. She had been harmed enough and probably hated men. He had read her all wrong. He thought, at first, that she had wanted him to spare Willie because she was carrying his child. But now he knew that she had only wanted to spare herself any guilt over his death. He shook his head. There was no way a man could know what was in another's heart. Debbie had lost everything in the world and the only reminder she had of her troubles was an unborn child growing inside her belly—a child she had not asked for nor wanted. And who would speak for the child when it was born? What kind of life would it have? Gunn knew well what people would say about Debbie when she gave birth. She had no ring on her finger, no folks to speak for her. Few men of worth would marry her under the circumstances, take the responsibility of raising a bastard.

Gunn heard the scream of a rabbit and knew that the hawk had made its kill. He looked out over the sun-scorched landscape and felt the heat shimmering up in waves. He stalked over to Duke, removed his hobbles. He led him down to the river, let him drink. He cut the hobbles on the halfbreed's horse and slapped him on the rump. Let the animal find its own way. Instead of heading toward Socorro, however, the horse headed south along the river. Someone would find it, strip the saddle off if nothing else. He didn't want to ride into Socorro leading a dead man's horse. He'd have problems enough without advertising himself.

Duke stood patiently for the saddle. Gunn cinched him up, put a knee to his belly and drew the last one tight. He helped Debbie with the linchpin and the oxen harness.

"You don't have to go back there with me," she said. "I'm obliged to you for burying Pa."

"Don't, Debbie. It's hard enough with you feeling like you do. I'm going back with you."

"You know there'll be trouble. If you go looking for that journal of Pa's, Larrabee will surely find out and sic his dogs on you."

He looked at her eyes. They were focused on a point beyond the oxen's head. She would not look at him.

"Debbie," he said quietly, "I know you've got a lot in your craw. But you can't change the past. Neither can I. You got a life to live and you don't want to make it any harder. I promised your pa I'd help you, look for his journal. I aim to keep those promises."

She looked at him then.

There was a flicker of understanding in their blue depths, but her jaw tightened and she looked away from him quickly. Gunn swung up into the saddle, waited for her to move the oxen.

"You do what you like," she said tersely and cracked a light whip over the oxen's backs. They moved and she turned them back toward the road.

Gunn stiffened, dug spurs into the horse's flanks. He rode up to the side of the wagon, grabbed the reins out of Debbie's hands, halted the oxen.

"Hold on a minute," he said. "You have a right to your grief, but not to condemn me out of hand. Not without an explanation."

The oxen bellered, switched their tails. Duke pawed the ground impatiently.

Debbie's face flushed, either from anger or embarrassment. She peered at Gunn from under the shade of her bonnet, her blue eyes misty.

"I know. You're probably wondering about last night. I was scared. I was lonely. I—I've had a lot of time to think about what I did with you. I think you probably took advantage of me, of—of my weakness. My pa told me some men would be that way. I reckon you figure I'm just easy. Well, I'm not, Mister Gunn. And I thank you to hand back my reins so I can get on with my business."

Gunn's face sagged with shock. As if Debbie had slapped him square on the cheek. He handed her the reins, pulled back on Duke's head. The horse backed up, away from the wagon.

Debbie cracked the thin buggy whip and the oxen lumbered off. Gunn sat there, watching the wagon rumble down the road. He took off his hat, scratched the back of his head. He had misjudged Debbie, it seemed. The way she described the night before wasn't at all the way it was. He hadn't taken advantage of her. Rather, it had been a mutual thing. A coming together of man and woman. No fetters, no dally on either of them. Yet now, she was acting as if he'd forced himself on her, as if he had raped her just as Willie Hadnot had done. Sometimes women didn't make much sense, but he'd never run across one as icy as Debbie had become. The shock of her father's death might have given her a loose cinch, or it could have been the way the half-breed had chosen to cash in his chips. Neither death was pretty, nor welcome. But death was a part of life and Debbie's reaction to it was hard to swallow. It was as if she blamed him for both of them. Or, maybe, he reasoned, it was only because he was the nearest, that he had to take the whipping.

The wagon topped the rise and started to disappear. Gunn looked up and then hunched down instinctively as a shot boomed.

He heard the hornet whine of the bullet passing high overhead. Then, Debbie's raw scream a moment later. The echoes hung like tattered rags in the air. A brief silence, then more gunshots, the bark of rifles and sixguns mixed together.

Gunn drew his rifle, kicked his horse in the flanks. He bent low over the saddle, levered a live round into the chamber of his Winchester. Shots blistered the air, whined from struck rocks. But no one was shooting at him. And, he could see no one. He reached the top of the slope and saw the oxen straining at their traces, barreling downhill, back toward the Rio Grande. He saw a man on horseback, some three or four hundred yards away. Saw a puff of smoke, heard the *crack* of the rifle seconds later. The road was a death trap!

Gunn reined Duke over hard, raced after Debbie in the wagon.

A pair of shots rang out, closer, and he caught a glimpse of men riding through saguaro, shooting from horseback.

The wagon reached the river, veered left. The left rear wheel hit a hump, tipping the wagon up high on that side. The load shifted and the wagon gave a lurch. To his horror, Gunn saw the wagon flip over.

66

The groan of metal and the twisting sound of wood reached his ears. The oxen spooked and dragged the wagon behind them as they ran along the bank. Gunn saw a flash of skirt and thought that Debbie might have been thrown clear. But he could not tell at that distance. He headed Duke toward the wagon, dragging along on its side, the canvas collapsed.

Shots fired the air around him.

There was no chance to return fire. His first thought was for Debbie. He gripped the rifle in his right hand, lay it hard against the pommel as Duke zig-zagged through the cactus, heading for the river.

The oxen stopped when the wagon wedged tight against a boulder. Their lowing was full of fear now.

Gunn saw two riders heading for the wagon at an angle, trying to cut him off. He worked the horse back and forth to avoid the shots of a man still up on the road, shooting down at him. Puffs of dirt and stone kicked up all around him as the rifleman tried to find his range.

The river came up fast and Gunn knew he had to make a stand.

He jumped off Duke, hit the ground running. Duke scratched hard to avoid falling into the river, wheeled and dashed downstream, trailing his reins.

The two horsemen separated, scatted for cover as Gunn stumbled to a halt, stood his ground. He brought his rifle up for a snap shot, fired, ran to a saguaro. He levered another bullet into the chamber, heard gunfire at less than a hundred yards away.

Bullets thunked into the cactus. A movement to his right caught Gunn's eye. He stepped back, took aim with the Winchester. Sunlight glinted from a rifle barrel as the man on horseback fired from the hip. Gunn fired quickly, knew he had missed just as his finger depressed the trigger. The horseman disappeared behind a cluster of rocks.

A shot from Gunn's left drew his attention away from the rifleman behind the rocks. A bullet tugged at his shirt and he heard the spent bullet spang into the river.

Gunn dropped to his knees, levered again.

There were at least three men shooting at him now. The man on the road had apparently joined the other two in trying to gun him down.

The man on his left dismounted, took to the brush before Gunn could get off a shot. Gunn's eyes sought his target: a bobbing hat, the glint of light on metal. He raised the rifle to his shoulder, tracked the bobbing hat.

Before he could fire, another shot rang out from somewhere above the second man.

Sand stung his eyes as a bullet plowed the earth a foot in front of him. Temporarily blinded, Gunn ducked, rubbed the grit from his eyes. For several seconds he was vulnerable. Shots blistered the air above his head. Finally, the grit loosened and he could see through tear-filled eyes.

He was in a bad spot. No question about that.

At least three men bearing down on him, all of them deadly shots. The brush around him was being chewed to bits by unerring rifle fire. It was only a question of time before one of the shooters found his mark.

Yet he had no place to run. Or hide.

He glanced up the bank, saw the overturned

wagon, the bawling oxen. A crumpled shape in the shadows might have been Debbie. If so, she was hurt. Or dead. He could expect no help there. It was all open ground from his spot to the wagon. They'd cut him down like scythed wheat if he tried to run for it.

Gunn looked behind him. At the river. The water swirled, a dark brown, wide and deep. He might make it into the river, but then what? He'd be a sitting duck in a barrel.

A shot seared a path inches from Gunn's ear. Smoke hung in the air forty yards away.

Gunn cracked off a shot, levered a live round. Getting low on rifle ammunition too. The rest of it in his saddlebags.

A low curse escaped his lips.

The bastards had him.

He would take one, maybe two of them with him.

Gunn flattened out, slid sideways in back of the saguaro. Let them find him. There was no place he could run. They'd have to come right on him to get him.

"Get him, Jake?" called one man.

The man behind the rocks. Only he wasn't there anymore. Somewhere in between.

"Dunno!" said a voice thirty, forty yards away. Slightly to the left of the saguaro.

"He's back there," said a third voice. Higher up, in between the other two. The man on the road, Gunn figured. Now come down to get in on the kill.

Gunn lay waiting. Listening.

A silence settled over the land.

The gunmen weren't shooting at random anymore. They had him where they wanted him. Surrounded, his back against a wall. Only the wall was the river and it was just as strong as rock for all practical purposes.

He reached down, checked his pistol. It was snug in its holster. He'd need it at close range. Meanwhile, the rifle might as well serve out its load. He had three or four shots left. Call it three, to be sure.

He peered out from the saguaro. Saw a hat crown thirty yards away. He brought the rifle up awkwardly, sighted the hat in. Squeezed off a shot. The hat sailed away.

A trick!

Bullets kicked up dirt and stone as three rifles blazed at once.

Gunn pulled his head back behind the cactus fast.

He worked the lever on the Winchester. The sound carried, he knew.

No more shots.

Gunn listened to the sound of his own breath.

They were moving closer. The three of them. He could feel their movement. Slow as snakes.

It was going to be pure hell in a minute.

A sound startled him.

Movement.

Gunn's eyes shifted to the wagon.

It lay there like a hulk, one side shattered, the other bellied up like some dead beast.

An arm waved above the shadowed shape.

A low moan reached his ears.

Debbie!

She was hurt. Hurt bad from the sound of her.

"Gunn?" Louder now.

70

"Shh!" he whispered.

"Help me! The baby . . . !"

Gunn's blood froze.

Debbie needed him. He was between a rock and a hard place for damned sure.

Again, she called out to him.

Gunn pulled his legs under him, stood up. He had to try. If it was the last thing he did, he had to try and help Debbie.

"Hold on!" he called.

Then he made his move. He fired as he raced from behind the towering saguaro. Gunfire erupted. Bright lights flashed. Something struck him in the head. A blue light danced. He felt himself staggering, his legs gone from under him. A warm wetness trickled down the side of his face.

The sun danced in the sky. The earth whirled beneath him. A blindness struck him as he fell away, the rifle shots dim pops in his cloudy brain. He felt himself falling, falling and he heard hoarse shouts of triumph somewhere far off in the distance.

And the blackness rushed up to meet him head on.

CHAPTER SIX

"Haw, Jake, you busted him clean!" shouted Gus Whitcomb, running toward the river.

"Blowed his head clean off, I'm thinking," said the other man, Nate Crumb.

Jake Early grinned in satisfaction as he stood up, twenty-five yards from where Gunn had been hit. He was the man who had ridden behind the rocks, sneaked up close for the killing shot.

Jake was a bowlegged man with a thick dark beard, handlebar moustache. His nose looked like a barrel-bung, flattened on the end, thick as a corncob. His dark eyes were buried under folds of flesh that receded away from the thick beard that grew high on his cheeks like black wool. He waddled down the slope, a thin curl of smoke spiraling from the end of his barrel.

Nate Crumb had been the man on the road. He was short, stocky, bald-headed, with a knife mark around his forehead that showed he'd been scalped once. He had pale blue eyes, a tattoo on his chest, Chinese-made in San Francisco a dozen years before. The tattoo, part of it, was always visible. It was an eagle with a snake in its mouth. His shirt was unbuttoned at the top so people could see the eagle's head and the snake.

Gus Whitcomb had light sandy hair, deep blue eyes that were strangely vacuous. He had teeth missing that gave him an oddly idiotic look when he smiled. He had a wad of tobacco lumping his jaw and he spat into the dirt as the three of them came together at the river bank. Gus stood taller than the other two men, but not by much. He was leaner and his breath reeked of cheap whiskey. A flask stuck out of his back pocket, shining in the sunlight.

The water was bloody next to the bank.

"You got him all right," Nate observed.

"Hmm. Mebbe," allowed Jake.

"Sheeit, he's plumb dead," avowed Gus. "No fuggin' doubt about it."

Jake's eyes scanned the river, looking for further evidence of his riflemanship. He saw nothing.

"Blood on the ground here," said Gus, looking down. "I saw his face. You got him in the head, sure as hell."

"All right," Jake grunted. "Let's see if that shit-heel Barnes is in the wagon."

"I heard that gal a-hollerin'," said Nate. "Look, there she is, a-lyin' in a heap."

The three men walked to the wagon, rifles at the ready. Jake glanced over his shoulder a time or two, still not satisfied. He'd feel a lot better if he could see the body of the man he had shot. He wondered who he was. Maybe the girl would know, or her old man, Caleb Barnes.

His head felt like an oversized melon. Throbbed

73

like a sumbitch. That damned Larrabee! Sending them back out when the breed didn't come back. Well, it turned out he was right. There was no sign of Willie and somebody had seen him riding back out this way early of the morning.

Debbie looked up at the three men with wet eyes. Her face was contorted in agony.

"Well, girlie," said Gus, taking the initiative, "looks like you had a accident for yourself. Your pa in the wagon?"

Nate looked through the tattered canvas.

"Nobody in here," he said.

"Well, girlie?" asked Gus. "Who was your friend?"

Debbie began to sob. The gunmen looked at each other. They shifted their feet uncomfortably.

"That man I kilt, friend of yours?" demanded Jake, stepping closer.

"Lay into her, Jake," said Nate.

Debbie stopped shaking, looking up at Jake defiantly. Her hatred showed plain.

These were the men responsible for her father's death. Indirectly, they were also responsible for the death of Willie Hadnot. And now they had murdered the man called Gunn. She felt terribly alone, vulnerable. Anger boiled up inside her, mingled with the pain in her belly. She felt as if her insides had been broken, thrown back together in the wrong places.

Debbie drew a deep breath as if to stifle her rage. She glared at Jake with tear-filled eyes. Her lips trembled. Her hands clutched her belly, shook with the tremors of anxiety. Her face was streaked and smeared with dirt, adding to her savage, bereft look.

74

"Well, where's your pa?" asked Jake. "Gettin' them feathers off'n his hide?"

"You killed him," Debbie hissed. "He's buried back up there."

Gus laughed harshly.

"Hear that, Nate? Barnes is dead. Saves us some grief at that."

"Don't you animals have any respect for the dead?" Debbie snapped. "Pa was a good man. Better'n the likes of Larrabee."

"Mind your tongue, girlie," said Jake. "Caleb got hisself into that fix and I reckon he paid for bein' a brick or two short of a load. Larrabee offered him a chance't to get on the right side. Caleb just had a hard-boned head is all."

Debbie spat at Jake.

He stepped back a pace, glanced at her.

"You watch you don't wind up side by side with your pa," he said, an ominous tone in his voice. "Now, you seen Willie Hadnot this day?"

"I saw him," Debbie said, smirking with satisfaction. "I saw him twice, in fact."

"Twice?"

"Once alive, once dead."

Jake's eyes sank back in the folds of flesh, narrowed to a porcine malevolence.

"The halfbreed dead?" asked Gus stupidly.

"That feller we shot do the job on Willie?" asked Nate.

Debbie nodded. The corners of her mouth curled upward slightly.

"Must of shot him in the back," said Gus, a trace of awe, or disbelief, in his voice.

"Yair," agreed Nate.

"That what happened?" pressed Jake. "He got the drop on Willie?"

"Willie snuck up on the man you shot. Thought he was asleep in his blanket. Willie shot into the blanket. I guess he got the drop on Willie at that. But it was a fair fight. Willie shot too. But the other man was faster. And he shot truer."

Debbie was gloating now, despite the pain. She couldn't help it. The expressions on the faces of the three men were stony, disbelieving. She wished Gunn were alive to see them. Whatever else Willie had been, the men had respected him. He was a good shot and he didn't back down. In fact, she believed that these men had been afraid of Willie.

"I don't believe her," said Gus. "Willie was one smart cat. He had eyes in the back of his head."

"Where's Willie buried?" asked Jake.

"He isn't buried. The man who killed him threw him into the river."

"You're lyin'." Jake stepped forward, his rifle raised as if to strike Debbie in the face. She cringed, moved backwards. A sharp pain shot through her abdomen and she paled.

"No!" Debbie gasped through clenched teeth. "It's the truth!"

"Who the hell was that *hombre* anyways?" asked Nate.

Jake lowered the rifle, but the anger lingered on his face like cloud shadows.

"Yeah, who was he?" Jake asked.

"He called himself Gunn."

"Gunn?"

76

"That's right. He was a good man. Kind. He tried to help my pa."

Jake turned to the other two men, a worried look in his eyes.

"Either of you heard the name before?"

Nate shook his head. Gus blinked stupidly.

"He the feller we heard about up in Coloraddy two, three years back?" Gus asked.

"Might be," said Jake. "And over to Wyoming."

"He's dead anyways, what's it matter?" asked Nate, who drifted toward the wagon. He ripped the canvas, looked inside as he peeled back the torn portion. "Man's dead anyways."

Jake sucked in a breath.

"Come on," he said curtly, "let's get this gal back to town. Nathaniel will want to talk to her. Gus, you fetch up that Gunn feller's hoss. Nate, you shoot them oxen or cut 'em loose."

"Hell, I'll drive 'em back to town. Worth a few dollars." Nate was inside the wagon, rummaging through the debris. His voice sounded as if he was in a cave.

"You do what you like, then," said Jake, feeling as if he had lost control. He didn't like what he had just heard. Gunn. The name rang a bell. A name spoken over campfires, in trail saloons, in bunkhouses late at night. A man he'd never seen, but heard of and wondered about. That business up in Colorado, for instance. On the Cache le Poudre. Man killed a whole bunch who had murdered his wife, then burned his own ranchhouse to the ground. What kind of man was that? And those stories out of Wyoming. Gunn again. Killing rustlers, putting

77

three shots in them neat as a whistle. Head, heart and gut. It took a mighty coldblooded bastard to do a thing like that. And he had cleaned out the rustlers, gone on his way. To where? Men spoke of him being in a lot of places. And they always talked like he was one mean sonofabitch and faster'n a greased pig in a mudslide.

Was that the man he had shot?

So easy? One shot to the head and him taking a dive into the river and never coming up? It was hard as hell to believe. For damned sure.

Jake felt a trickle of sweat rolling down his back. Itching his spine. He didn't like it here anymore. There was the smell of death in the air. It was too quiet. Too damned spooky. He jumped a foot when Nate yelled from deep in the bowels of the wagon.

"Hoo Haw! Looky what I found!"

"Dammit, Nate, keep it down!" Jake snapped.

Nate climbed out of the wagon, beaming. He held up Willie's pistol and gunbelt, the knife dangling in its sheath from the leather strap.

"Willie's gunbelt. She ain't lyin'! That jasper had to shoot Willie dead to get these. And now they're mine!"

"You're a born scavenger, Nate," said Jake.

Gus rode up a few minutes later, leading their horses, Gunn's. Nate had cut the oxen out of their traces, haltered them with ropes. Jake looked at him in disgust. He'd be five hours getting those animals back to Socorro.

"Kin you get up on a horse by yourself?" Jake asked Debbie.

She shook her head.

"Just leave me here," she said. "Tell Larrabee I got killed or something."

"No, you're goin'," said Jake. He shoved his rifle in its boot, walked over to her. He grabbed her elbow, pulled her up to her feet. She swooned and he caught her in his arms.

"Fainted," said Gus. Jake snorted, carried the unconscious girl over to Gunn's horse, lay her across the saddle, face down.

"Have to tie her down," Jake said.

"Likely she won't make it that way. You better carry her," said Gus, offering no help.

Jake saw that Gus was probably right. For once. He cursed, climbed up behind the cantle. He lifted Debbie to a sitting position, slid into the saddle. He let her drop into his lap. She didn't weigh much, but it was all dead weight. He put an arm around her waist, let her head sag to one side.

"You lead my hoss, Gus," Jake said. "I'll ride this'n in to Socorro."

"How about Nate?"

"Let him take his damned time!" growled Jake. It was a long ride carrying a sack of meal in his arms. He kicked Duke, the horse moved out easily.

They left Nate behind, Gus riding out leading Jake's horse. Nate spent a half hour trying to lead the oxen, then shot them both between the eyes in disgust. He galloped hard, trying to catch up to the other two men, cursing himself for a fool.

But he had Willie Hadnot's pistol and knife in his saddlebags.

That was better than nothing.

* * *

Nathaniel Larrabee stood on the porch of *The Hog and Keg,* pulling on a cigar. The thumb of his left hand was hooked into a vest pocket, near the butt of his pistol. Nat was left-handed and he never carried anything in his left hand. He was a tall, florid-faced man with groomed sideburns, a moustache that drooped slightly. His clothes were immaculate, tailored for him in San Francisco. They seemed out of place in the dusty, ramshackle trail town, but in front of *The Hog and Keg,* with its Barbary Coast false front, they seemed not at all incongruous.

Larrabee looked down the street, frowned. He blew a plume of smoke out of one side of his mouth, pulled his hat brim lower to shade his hazel eyes from the afternoon sun. Few people were about on that hot afternoon. It was quiet down the street at the Rio Queen, but as always, there were a few men in both places, drinking beer or whiskey, playing cards and dominoes. A rider had come in twenty minutes ago and told him about Jake and the others headed for town. With Deborah Barnes. Not her father, just Deborah. It was just as well. Caleb had been a hard head and with him out of the way, Larrabee's secret was safe.

He hadn't found the journal, though, and that bothered him. Nate Crumb had been ordered to go through that wagon with a fine-toothed comb, but he knew it hadn't been in the wagon. His men had thrown the stuff in the night they had tarred and feathered Caleb, had gone over the wagon carefully, looking for false boxes. The notebook, or journal, whatever it was, had either been hidden at the house or at Lorna Starr's place. But last night he'd had men ransack Lorna's rooms. He half expected her to come storming up the street at any minute accusing him of the deed. But he had an alibi.

Nat Larrabee didn't do things by half degree.

Caleb had stumbled on to his true identity. There was no doubt about that. Instead of using it against him, however, he had kept his mouth shut. Asked only to be left alone. But that wasn't Larrabee's way. Caleb could ruin him. And he probably would have too, since he was a writer. He wouldn't have been able to sit on that deadly information for very long without trying to get it into print.

Well, maybe the girl knew where the journal was. In all likelihood, her pa was dead and buried. His secret, damn him, with him. The man said that she was riding with Jake on another man's horse, a dun. That was a curious note in itself. Something had happened out there since the man had said nothing about Willie Hadnot being with Jake. Nor anything about Willie's horse, though Nat had questioned him carefully.

Larrabee saw the pale dun come into view. Saw Jake's beard, the girl in his lap. Behind him, Crumb and Whitcomb. Whitcomb was trailing Jake Early's horse.

Nat threw the cigar out into the street, took his thumb out of his vest pocket. It was almost four in the afternoon.

The riders pulled up and puffs of dust blew away from the horses' hooves.

Debbie was awake, grimacing in pain.

"Caleb's dead, the girlie's hurt," said Jake.

"Good afternoon, Miss Barnes," said Larrabee politely. "I'm sorry for the inconvenience."

"I hate you, Larrabee," she said grimly. "I hate you pure."

Larrabee smiled condescendingly and stepped down from the porch. Curious passersby looked at the assemblage and hurried on by. Larrabee ignored them.

"You must be tired, my dear, and probably hungry too. Jake you bring the little lady inside. Take her up to my rooms."

Debbie started to protest, but Larrabee stepped up close so that only she and Jake could hear what he had to say.

"I don't want any trouble here," he said. "You behave and you'll be treated well."

"Like my pa?"

"Your pa was a fool." Larrabee shot Jake a look. "Get her upstairs, Jake."

Too weak to protest, Debbie allowed Jake to take her off of Gunn's horse and up the steps. Just before she went inside the saloon and gambling parlor, she saw a group of people coming up the street. She recognized one of them as Lorna Starr. She stopped in her tracks, started to turn and go back out in the street, but Jake pushed her on inside.

"You must mind you do what you're told, girlie," said Jake, forcing her toward the stairs that led to Larrabee's quarters.

Lorna Starr passed the Rio Grande Hotel, walking toward Larrabee with long strides. She held her skirts up out of the dust. Following her were two men and a woman who worked for her.

"Here comes trouble," said Gus under his breath.

"Get the horses to the stables," Larrabee ordered. "I'll handle this."

Gus and Nate started toward the livery, passing Lorna and her entourage. She gave them a withering glance with sea-green eyes that were fiery as emeralds.

"Nathaniel Larrabee, who was that just went in your place?" Lorna demanded. She was a tall, leggy woman, with auburn hair that looked like spun copper as the sun's rays burnished the curly locks. She wore a long-skirted gingham dress, practical shoes, a locket around her neck on a velvet band. She called these simple clothes her "dailies," because she dressed more extravagantly at night when she oversaw the doings at her saloon, *The Rio Queen*. She stopped a few paces from Larrabee and spat out a strand of hair caught in the corner of her mouth. Deep dimples framed her lips. Her nose was straight and thin; her teeth white as polished snow marble.

"Why, a friend, Lorna," said Larrabee smoothly. "Just a friend."

"It looked like Deborah Barnes."

"I don't see how that would concern you, Lorna."

"I heard what your boys did to Caleb. I demand to see Debbie if she's inside."

"I'm afraid that's not possible. Besides, it wouldn't be healthy for you to go in the Hog and Keg. We have some mighty randy boys bellied up to the bar."

Lorna frowned. She was outmaneuvered, but

83

undaunted. Besides, she had come to see Larrabee on another matter. Her eyes narrowed. She put her hands on her hips, stepped two paces closer to Larrabee.

"I'll let that matter go by, for the moment, Nathaniel. What I came to see you about was the destruction of my property."

"I haven't the slightest idea what you're talking about, Lorna."

"No? I think so. My rooms were ransacked. I think you or your men sneaked in and rummaged through my things. Why? What could I possibly have that you would want? Besides the Rio Queen, that is."

"There you have it," said Larrabee glibly. "There's nothing you have that I would want. Probably one of your underpaid employees took your rooms apart."

Lorna fumed, but she had no proof. She was frankly puzzled. Larrabee had given her a rough time, but whatever he was looking for in her rooms was something she wasn't aware of having. And now he was as cool as ever. She hated him at that moment, but realized her own frustrations were getting the upper hand. She hated to back down, but she couldn't give her enemy the satisfaction of seeing her lose control.

"I'll get you for this, Nathaniel. If it's the last thing I do."

She turned on her heel and left as Gus strolled across the street. Nate Crumb was still at the livery.

Larrabee waited for Gus, pulling a cigar out of his inside coat pocket. He watched Lorna going back to the Rio Queen, frowning as he thought of her threat.

"Let's have it all, Gus," he said. "Where's Willie, for one thing."

Gus told him what he knew. When he mentioned the name Gunn, Larrabee stiffened.

"You sure this Gunn is dead?" he asked.

"Sure as your name's Nathaniel Larrabee," said Gus, grinning idiotically.

Larrabee's face darkened into a scowl. That was just the trouble.

His name wasn't Nathaniel Larrabee.

CHAPTER SEVEN

Gunn felt his feet go out from under him. The dark explosion in his head cleared momentarily just as he fell into the waters of the Rio Grande. He heard a distant splash as his rifle hit the water. Then, he was under water, his lungs miraculously full of air.

The shock revived him.

His head throbbed mercilessly.

He opened his eyes, saw the murky water. He went deep, deeper still. His lungs ached, but he realized that to surface would be suicide.

The current grabbed at him, swirled him still deeper. He knew he would have to swim in order to stay under, keep from being tossed around like a cork. His pistol weighed him down. His boots felt as if they had been filled with lead.

The current pulled him downstream. Fast. By swimming with it, he put yards and yards between him and his pursuers. He didn't think about them now, only about the burning in his lungs. He had to go far enough downstream to surface, take another breath.

The water was filled with debris, minute particles

of plants, twigs, leaves.

Hours seemed to go by. He felt as if he was swimming in slow motion.

He fought off the panic that rose up in him as he realized that he wasn't in control anymore. The deep current was strong. His boots and gunbelt were weighing him down.

Fire blazed in his lungs.

Struggling only worsened his condition. The darkness swirled in his brain again. It would be so easy now to give up. Open his mouth, take in a breath. Die. Water would rush into his lungs and he would sink to the bottom.

For a second or two, he considered it. His head didn't hurt so much now. The pain was dull, far away. Blood trickled into his eye and then was swirled away by the water.

He looked up, saw the murky sunlight playing on the surface.

Kicking hard, Gunn struggled to reach the surface. Air. Oxygen for his tortured lungs. He pulled with leaded arms, kicked with waterlogged boots weighing down his feet and legs. The sunlight seemed far away, out of reach. The blackness threatened to engulf him again as he groped through the murky waters. The silt stung his eyes, the current pulled him down. His lungs seemed at the point of bursting. Yet if he let the air out this far down, he would not have enough strength to get to the surface. He would gulp in water, and drown.

The surface drew away from him as a strong undercurrent tugged him downward. He closed his eyes and flailed at the water. His arms felt as if they had anvils tied to them. His feet moved as if they were attached to pig weights.

Yet to give up now was against his nature. He was alive. If he let his breath out slowly, the searing fire in his lungs would ease. But after that, he would either have to surface or suck in the deadly water that surrounded him in a pale haze.

Gunn stopped straining. He let the current tumble him, swirl him farther downstream. The seconds trailed by, as long as hours. Yet, he didn't sink. Instead, he felt an uplifting surge of current roll up underneath him, bear him close to the surface. He opened his eyes, saw the dim outlines of a bank. The water had undercut the bank, churned back into the stream at a bend. This was the current that was bearing him up to lifegiving air on the surface.

He pulled at the water, first with one hand, then the other, using them like scoops. He kicked against the current and his face broke the surface. He blew out the stale burning air in his lungs and gulped in water and oxygen. He gagged, strangled, but the pain eased. He spluttered and coughed. Took in a fresh draught of new air. This time, his head was high enough above the water so that he didn't swallow any of it.

He looked back upstream, saw only the tops of hats and then the current whipped him around the bend. He tried to make it to the shore, but the waters grabbed at him, sucked him under. This time, he paddled hard to stay close to the surface. His gunbelt weighed a ton around his waist. His boots were sodden ballasts.

Gunn managed to keep his head above water

through vigorous paddling and kicking. But his strength was ebbing fast. He fought the current, trying to push himself toward the west shore. The river was deceptive. On the surface it appeared to be a gentle, almost lazy, stream. But the current was swift, cantankerous. Gunn considered taking off his boots and gunbelt, but knew this to be a foolish consideration. If he reached the shore, he'd be barefoot and unarmed. In this country, that could be fatal. No, he'd need his boots and pistol if he was going to get out of his predicament alive. There were three men back there, all armed and dangerous. No telling what they might do to Debbie. He shuddered to think about it. She was hurt, that was certain. They might kill her, or they might take her back into town, try to find Caleb's journal. He had to try and stop them, even though he might have to walk miles. They would surely take his horse, so he'd be afoot. It was a long walk back to Socorro. Hard enough in boots not made for walking; harder still without any protection for his feet.

Muscles twinged in Gunn's legs, threatened to lock up with cramps. His lungs burned now with the exertion of breathing. His arms were numb logs attached to his shoulders. The *splash-splash* of his hands on the water seemed a disconnected sound as if someone else was making the noise. Blood dripped down his face and his head throbbed as the sun hammered down on the wound. At times he couldn't see if he was making any headway or not. The shore seemed to come close, then pull away tauntingly. Once or twice, he gulped in water, strangled. Lifting his head up with a superhuman effort, he coughed out the water, drew in air.

The current eased as Gunn slogged closer to the bank, moving his arms and legs now through sheer willpower. He no longer felt any sensation in his arms or hands. His hips ached. His legs were numb leaden things.

A spear of pain drove through his skull.

Gunn stopped kicking, exhausted.

His legs sank and he knew he was going to go down. Once he stopped kicking, he knew he would never be able to summon enough strength to get them going again. His arms now were supporting all of his weight in the water. The muscles in his shoulders tightened up into steel bands that wouldn't respond to his mental commands.

Gunn felt himself sinking.

Vainly, he struggled to kick himself back to the surface. Sharp pains gripped his legs. He flailed the water in a last-ditch attempt to stay afloat. His legs stopped moving, heavy as a pair of waterlogged stumps.

He saw the shore. So close, yet so far away. Tufts of grass growing on the banks. Saguaro dotting the land a stone's throw away. And something else. An animal, standing a few yards away downstream, staring at him.

The halfbreed's horse!

The sorrel gelding seemed amused to see Gunn's head floating toward the bank, his hands clawing at the water in desperation.

It was all over.

Gunn let himself sink, his legs gone dead. No feeling in his arms. His hands useless appendages

90

with numb fingers.

He took in a deep breath and closed his eyes.

He thought about the strange way he was cashing in. All alone, with no eyes on him, but a dead man's horse. Nothing but river and sky, cactus and rolling land a million miles away. It was an empty, peaceful feeling. He gritted his teeth, opened his eyes and wondered why he hadn't sunk underneath the water. The sky had never looked bluer, the cactus more stately. The sorrel gelding ambled down to the bank, lowered his head to drink. Swatted flies with its dark tail. Nickered to him.

Gunn felt something. A sensation far down his leg. His feet. Sliding on a rock, heels digging into mud.

A rock! Mud!

He had touched bottom!

Gunn stood up, his legs shaking. The water swirled around him, chest high.

He grinned, took a breath.

The bank was no more than a half dozen paces away. The river eddied here, and he knew he could make it. All he had to do was think about moving his legs. About walking!

His feet moved, the soles of his boots sliding off of slimy stones, oozing through mud. But they moved.

Gunn felt the pressure of the water slide off his chest as the river got shallower. He lunged for the bank, impeded by the water. He slipped, but did not go under. Close now, he took his time. Finally, he reached a point just off the bank. His boots broke the suction-hold of the mud and he pitched forward onto the shore. Recovering, he sogged up onto the bank, dripping wet. His feet squished inside his boots. He lay down, too exhausted to go any further. He let the hot sun blaze over his drenched clothes. He felt the water leaking out of his boots, trickling onto the ground. He lifted one leg straight up in the air. Water cascaded down his leg.

Gunn laughed weakly.

He let the leg down, raised the other one.

Ten pounds lighter. At least.

His buckskins clung to his body. He was glad they were as thin as they were. The water had not weighted them down too much. Gunn drew his pistol. He ejected the five bullets, pulled out the bail money from the sixth cylinder. He laid the three ten dollar bills out to dry in the sun. They were damp only on the edges except for one that was soaked through. He lay the pistol on a clump of grass to dry, as well.

He sat up, took off his boots, wrung out his socks.

He saw his hat on the shore a few yards away. It must have beat him there by a few minutes.

The sorrel had finished drinking, was moseying his way, dragging its reins. The horse walked in a sideways fashion, sidling up to him warily.

Gunn spoke soothingly to the animal.

Gingerly, he felt his head, tracing a finger over and around the wound.

"Lucky," he mused aloud.

The wound was slight. Clean. The bullet had creased him. He'd have a furrow in his skull for a while, but the blood would clot and the wound would heal. The bone was tender underneath.

The horse moved closer, head cocked to one side,

the whites showing in its eyes.

"Could have been worse," Gunn said, his voice low.

The horse nickered.

Gunn continued to talk to it as if it was another human. When the horse got close enough, Gunn grabbed a rein, but did not pull on it. He took up the slack slowly, then reached out a hand slowly. He opened his palm, let the horse lick the salt from his hand. He bent his fingers way back so that if the horse decided to bite he wouldn't lose them. The horse didn't bite, but continued to lap at the moisture on Gunn's palm.

Gradually, feeling returned to Gunn's limbs. He petted the horse on its nose, its face.

"You're going to take us back upriver, hoss," he said. "Maybe find Duke and see what happened to the lady."

The horse jerked its head, spooking suddenly. Gunn held the rein tight, reached for the other one. He looked down at the river. He thought the gelding might have spooked at his hat, which was still there, moving slightly as water gently nudged it snug against the bank.

His eyes went beyond his hat to another object.

The bloated body of Willie Hadnot was downstream a few yards, sprawled next to the bank. His black hair floated in the water. His face was buried in mud, half of it anyway.

It was time to go. Gunn stood up, checked his pistol. He would oil it later, He reloaded, shoved it loosely back in its holster. He put his boots back on. They were still wet inside, and so were his socks.

Uncomfortable, but he was whole. He led the horse down the bank, retrieved his hat. It was sodden, but would dry in the wind once he forked Willie's horse.

He pulled himself up in the saddle. The horse started to buck, but Gunn slapped its withers, pulled the reins to show who was in command. The horse settled down and Gunn kicked him into motion. Heading back upstream.

Gunn approached the hulk of the broken wagon cautiously.

Where were the oxen?

He rode around the wagon, satisfied himself that Debbie was not there. He dismounted, studied the tracks very carefully. He put the story together. They had caught up his horse, put Debbie in the saddle with one of the men. One man had cut the oxen loose, led them up to the road. Hard going all the way.

Gunn walked back down to the wagon, suddenly hungry. But he would not stop to eat, even if there was food in the halfbreed's saddlebags or in the wagon. Instead, he walked to the bank where he'd been shot and peered down into the murky water. He saw nothing. But he knew it was there, unless someone had gone in after it. He sat down, took off his boots and socks, waded into the river. When he felt it with his foot, he stooped down and fished out the Winchester. Water ran out of the barrel as he lifted it. He shook it good, waded back to the bank. He sat down, worked the lever. One bullet came out. That was all he had left in the magazine.

It had been close. He was lucky to be alive.

Somebody thought he was already dead.

Three men.

He had a pretty good idea who they worked for. He could find out their names later. If he could find Debbie. If they hadn't killed her. Chances were that they had taken her back to Socorro to talk to Larrabee. He doubted if the gambler would harm a woman. At least not in town, where eyes could see. He tried to summon up a picture of Larrabee, but there was no way of knowing how he looked, what kind of a man he was. If he hadn't found the journal that Caleb had hidden under the stove, then that would give him additional background. He'd like to find the journal before he started looking for Debbie. Trouble was he didn't know where Barnes had lived.

Well, it worked both ways.

Larrabee didn't know what he looked like either. The only giveaway would be the halfbreed's horse. Somehow, he'd have to get rid of that before he went into town. That way, he'd have half a chance in finding out where Debbie was and what the journal contained.

Gunn shook the Winchester again. It was still wet. He'd have to clean and oil it later on. He put on his socks and boots. The socks were almost dry, baked by the boiling sun. They felt better anyway. He rammed the rifle into the saddle boot and mounted the sorrel.

A half hour later he passed the two oxen.

Flies swarmed up from their dead eyes. They had begun to bloat and Gunn smelled the ripeness of rotting meat. His pale eyes scanned the countryside. His hunger left him suddenly, replaced by a slow-fused anger.

The oxen had been shot in the head. Both of them. No matter that the beasts were valuable. It was a senseless taking of life. Gunn studied the tracks around the oxen, taking note of the horse's hoof-marks. The right front shoe was worn on the outer edges. The left rear shoe had an indentation in it, big enough to make an impression. He would be able to spot the horse by its shoes. If it came to that.

He hoped it would.

Gunn rode on, headed for Socorro.

The countryside was bleak, vacant, except for the saguaros, the rocks, the lizards basking in the sun. The sky was clear and blue as painted pottery, but the buzzards had already started to circle over the oxen, and farther downstream, they picked up the scent of Willie Hadnot.

If Willie was the best Larrabee had to offer, that wasn't enough.

Gunn had blood in his eye.

For Caleb Barnes, made to die a humiliating death from chicken feathers and tar.

For Debbie Barnes, kidnapped, an orphan, probably hurt.

And for himself, because he hated men who took what they wanted without regard for others' rights. He hated them for chasing down a helpless girl and ragging a man to death without a hearing or a fair fight.

He wanted blood.

In Socorro, he aimed to get it.

And the odds were hard.

At least four men that he knew of. Men with no

faces. Only three with names: Nat Larrabee, their leader; and the two Debbie had mentioned, Gus Whitcomb and Jake Early.

The fourth man would get his name on a bullet as well.

And a grave in Boot Hill!

* * *

The sorrel ran a thorn through its hoof five miles out of Socorro.

Gunn cursed and dismounted.

And then he began to think that it was Providence.

The horse was a death notice anyway. Probably known in town as belonging to the halfbreed. Certainly known to Larrabee and his men.

But he'd gone lame about four and a half miles too soon.

Gunn led the animal off the road, stripped him of bridle, saddle, saddlebags and boot. He found Winchester ammunition, loaded up his rifle, crammed a dozen more bullets into his shirt pocket. Hid the tack under several bushes, whopped the sorrel on the butt with the saddle blanket and ran him off toward the Rio Grande.

Then Gunn set out on foot, cross-country, avoiding the road.

The sun was falling off in the western sky and the shadows were long. Good enough. Night was a better time for a stranger on foot. He had questions to ask, people to size up. He tried to remember the town, but he had ridden around it without stopping. Maybe he'd had the feeling then. That it was not a good town. You got hunches, sometimes. About towns. About people. Socorro had looked like a trap. You go in, hunker up to the bar, and someone buys you a drink, starts asking questions. Next thing you know, you've either got trouble or have to ride on. Sometimes, just the name, his name, could bring the looks, the uneasy coughs, the wariness among strangers.

Trail towns could be deadly.

And this one was drawing him back like a moth to a candle.

Gunn let the sun go down.

He watched the lamps wink on in Socorro.

It was time.

Time to go in and find the man he was seeking.

Then it was kill or be killed.

Boot Hill didn't care about a man's name. There was room for one and all.

CHAPTER EIGHT

Gunn walked carefully up to the jacal, rifle in hand.

"*Información, por favor,*" he called quietly. "*Una pregunta, nada mas.*"

"*Quien es?*" called a voice from inside the hut.

"*Nadie que conoces. Un amigo, no mas.*" He didn't want to give out his name. Not yet. Even this poor hovel could hide someone who worked for Larrabee, or who was loyal to him for some reason. Gunn had picked out this particular adobe because it was set some ways from the main part of the trail and town. Also, they had no dog, which was unusual. Just a few chickens and a small, dried-up garden patch. Hard-scrabble place from the looks of it.

A small child peered out from the doorway. Ragged dress, bare feet. The voice who had replied was a woman's.

"*Mamá, mamá, aqui hay un gringo. Tiene un rifle.*"

"*No importa,*" said Gunn. "*Dejame a hablar con su mamá, niña.*"

99

The woman came to the door, stood just behind the small girl. She had a large butcher knife in her hand.

Gunn leaned the rifle against his leg, took off his hat.

"Do you speak English?" he asked.

"I speak," said the woman coldly.

"I'm looking for a friend's house," said Gunn. "Can you direct me?"

"Who is your frien'?"

"Caleb Barnes. He didn't tell me where he lived. Only in Socorro."

The woman disappeared suddenly. Pale lamplight backlit the small girl's hair. She stood there, staring at him. Gunn heard voices, talking rapidly in Spanish. One was a man's. Gunn put his hat back on, picked up his rifle. He smiled at the *niña*. The voices stopped.

A man came outside, bareheaded, his shirt open. He wore the pants of the *peones*, white, and sandals.

"What is it you want?"

"Some information. The house of Caleb Barnes. If you know him, where he lives."

"He is not there any more."

Gunn saw that the Mexican was looking at him carefully. In the dark, with the light behind him, Gunn could not see his eyes. But he knew he was being sized up. The woman was not in sight, but Gunn figured that she was back of her man, probably with a pistol in her hand. He debated on whether or not to take the Mexican into his confidence. It could complicate matters. Or it could make things easier.

"I know," said Gunn quietly. "The man is dead. Tarred and feathered. Killed by a man named Larrabee."

There it was. Gunn let his words settle like a stone thrown into a pool. If the man was on Larrabee's side he would let Gunn know. If he knew of Caleb's troubles, he would respond in a different way. He heard the Mexican suck in a breath, hold it.

"Who are you?" the Mexican asked finally.

"I was with Caleb when he died. With him and his daughter. My name is Gunn."

The Mexican stepped closer. Behind him, the woman appeared, an old pistol in her hand. Gunn smelled food cooking. His stomach winced with hunger.

"Put the pistol away, woman," the Mexican barked in Spanish, without turning around. To Gunn, he said: "You will find much trouble in this place if you go to the house of Caleb Barnes. There are men guarding the ashes."

"Ashes?" Gunn felt a queasy slide in his stomach, as if he'd swallowed a lizard dipped in oil.

"The house burned down this very afternoon, *señor*. Everyone went and looked at it. It was a very big fire and no one put any water on it. There is not much water here for such things, but no one even tried. Men were there with guns and they watched the house burn down while they made jokes and made water on the little flames. There is no house there anymore. There are only men waiting there until the ashes cool."

101

"Why?"

But Gunn already knew. So they could look for a strong box full of burnt papers. Or to make sure there were not any papers.

The Mexican shrugged.

"I'd still like to know where the house is and I will see to it that you do not have trouble over this. What is your name?"

"I am called Juan Yglesia. Please, you come inside my small house."

Gunn followed Juan into the house. The small child retreated, hid behind her mother's skirts. Juan introduced Gunn to his wife, Corazón, and his daughter, Charita, who was six years old. There were only two rooms in the hovel. A kitchen with a wood stove made from scrap, a table and chairs, and barrels made into storage bins and cupboards. The other room was laid out with sleeping pallets and religious objects on a small table and on the walls. The dirt floor was swept clear of food scraps and chicken offal. The smell of food was overwhelming.

"We will eat," said Juan, "and you will tell me why you will go to the house of *Señor* Barnes."

Juan, Gunn learned, was a worker in a leather shop. He tanned hides, made boots, saddles, holsters, sandals, quirts, whips, and the like. His hands were rough and strong. He did not make much money, but he enjoyed his work. The work was slow now until the winter when the hunters would bring in hides, the wagons cow and pig hides after the fall slaughter in the East.

Gunn told them, sparing the gory details, of what

102

had happened at the river. He told them of the promise he had made to Caleb, and how he had been shot and left for dead, managing to catch up the half-breed's horse and make it this far.

"The girl you speak of is at The Hog & Keg, but the Queen of Socorro is going to take her from that place."

"Who is she?"

"She is called Lorna Starr."

"The one Caleb worked for—owns The Rio Queen."

"Yes. She does not like this Larrabee. I heard her talking in the Rio when I was there a while ago having *una copa*. There was much talk and then the house of *Señor* Barnes caught fire and everyone went to see it burn."

"So you don't know if Miss Starr has seen Debbie Barnes."

Juan shook his head. He pushed away from the table, offered Gunn a cigar. It was a sign to leave the house, talk away from Juan's wife and his daughter. Gunn thanked Corazón and patted Charita on the head. The small girl giggled and dipped her head shyly.

Outside, Juan lit Gunn's cigar. The two men smoked. Stars winked in the sky and Gunn smelled woodsmoke. The town was quiet, from this distance, and looked to be smaller than it was. Chickens pecked at the dirt, clucked quietly. Juan shooed them away, walked out of earshot of his wife inside their kitchen.

"You will find nothing at the house," Juan said.

"Not tonight. In the morning, the guards will be asleep."

"How do you know?"

In the glow from Juan's cigar, Gunn saw a grin spread over the Mexican's face.

"Because they will be drunk. *Muy borracho.* I saw one of them bring two bottles to those on guard."

"Was Larrabee there?"

"He was there. Everybody was there."

"What kind of man is he, Juan?"

Juan shrugged. "He is a man who makes money. He likes to be the boss. I stay out of his saloon."

"Know where he came from?"

"No. No one knows that. People do not ask. It's funny, though. *Señor* Barnes asked me the same thing. A long time ago. He asked a lot of people. I think that is not a good question to ask. Another man, before Barnes came here, asked that same question. He, too, is dead."

Gunn's eyebrows went up. He held the cigar away from his face, tapped the ashes from the glowing end.

"How did he die?"

"They said he got drunk and killed himself. But I don't believe that."

"Why?"

"It would be very hard to shoot yourself in the back of the head, no?"

Gunn finished his cigar.

"I need to go to a hotel for the night, I reckon," he told Juan. "But I don't want to make anyone curious."

"There is only one hotel, the Rio Grande. *Señorita* Starr has rooms, and so does Larrabee. But you should stay at the house of my sister. She can help you if you want to look at the house of Barnes. I will take you there."

"Where does she live?"

"Across the street from where the house of Barnes once stood."

"I don't want to impose on your sister."

"She will want to see you. She was married to a *gringo*. His name was Lorenzo Miller. He was a lawman. The last lawman in Socorro. My sister, she loved that man and she has hatred for Larrabee. Much hatred."

"How did her husband die?"

"He is the man I told you about. The one who was asking questions about Larrabee. He was a smart man, but he did not live very long."

"You mean he's the one they said committed suicide?"

"That is the one. Come, we will go to the house of my sister. I think you are the man she has been looking for to come to Socorro."

* * *

Juan Yglesia knocked on the back door of the small frame house. The porch was dark, but bronze light leaked from around the shade. Gunn heard footsteps inside the house, boards creaking. He had already seen the two men across the street, smelled

105

the smouldering ashes of what once was Caleb Barnes' home. The guards were talking and drinking. The glow from their cigarettes served to define their positions. They sat against trees a few feet from each other. The street was quiet.

"*Quien es?*" came a woman's voice from inside the house.

"Juan. *Abre la puerta.*"

The door opened a few inches.

Gunn saw a shadowy face break into a smile. Juan and his sister exchanged greetings. He heard his own presence being explained in Spanish. A moment later he was inside, the door locked behind him.

"This is my sister, Monica," said Juan. "She has said you can stay this night with her. There is a bedroom for guests."

"I'm most grateful, ma'am," said Gunn.

"So, you are Gunn," said Monica. "Come, I want to talk to you. Juan, would you like a *copa?*"

"No, I did not tell Corazón I was coming here. She will be wondering where we had went to, I think."

"You, Juan. Corazón would not approve of this and you are a little sneak. Go on back and tell her the lie you have made up."

Monica spoke with laughter in her voice. Gunn could feel the strong bond between this sister and brother. He could not see Monica's face very well, but her speech was cultured, faintly accented, and he knew she had long dark hair, a heart-shaped face. The lampglow from the livingroom showed only the barest outlines of her figure.

Juan left quickly, laughing quietly to himself.

106

Gunn realized that Monica had his hand in hers and was leading him down the hall as if he was a small boy and she had just taken charge of him.

In the light, he saw her plain.

She was taller than Juan by several inches. He couldn't determine her age, but she looked to be no more than twenty-five or twenty-six. Perhaps closer to thirty. She was beautiful, with almond eyes of burnished brown, long eyelashes, raven-black hair, a dazzling smile, shapely figure with flaring hips and trim legs. She had a dimple in her chin, dimples when she smiled. She wore a white flower in her hair, a brown-eyed Susan held in place with a thin ribbon. Her bodice was low-cut, revealed ample breasts, a slim waist. She wore a gay skirt laced with dark ribbon that was cut full, high enough to show off her shapely ankles.

"Please sit down, Gunn," she said. "Will you have some *aguardiente?* You must be exhausted coming back from the dead like Lazarus."

"Huh?" Gunn took off his hat, stood awkwardly, gazing at Monica's beauty. She had caught him totally by surprise.

"Sit down," Monica smiled. "I wasn't expecting you, but I'm glad you're here. I work at the Hotel. The Rio Grande. I spoke to Debbie Barnes before I got off. She told me you were dead. Shot by a man named Jake Early."

Gunn sank to a chair, even more surprised than before. He felt as if he'd fallen into a giant spider web that was connected to everyone he'd met or heard about in the last few days. At the center of the web

107

was a man he'd never seen: Nat Larrabee.

Without asking him again, Monica went to a cabinet, opened it and selected a bottle of brandy. She poured the liquid into two small snifters. Gunn looked around the room. There was a fireplace and he saw that the house had originally been adobe, but had been framed with wood. There was a rifle over the fireplace, another leaning next to the door. One of the chairs was turned to the front window next to the door. The shades were pulled. The lamp stood on a table in the center of the room. Brightly woven Navajo blankets adorned the couch. The chair he sat in was covered with cowhide. It was a man's room, yet there was a woman's touch as well. Doilies here and there, a vase with flowers. Tintypes on the walls, some paintings that were amateurish but strong in their use of color and line. A footstool in front of the chair he sat in, also covered with cowhide.

"Drink this slowly," said Monica. "It's pure fire. Not what you'd buy at the Hog & Keg."

Again, that smile of hers. The dimples. The wise sparkling eyes. It was obvious that Monica knew a lot more than he did about the situation. It was a stroke of good luck picking out Juan's *jacal* among all the others. He was riding a streak, for sure.

The brandy tasted fine. It burned all the way down, but didn't tear up his stomach. He smiled at Monica, tossed his hat down next to the chair. He didn't put his feet up on the footstool. He watched as Monica glided to the chair by the window, turned it around. She sat down, facing him, put her glass on the table next to the chair.

She looked at Gunn, then at the rifle by the door.

"I was watching those men over there," she explained. "I don't trust them. They're half drunk now and know I live here. I wouldn't hesitate to shoot them dead if they came over here."

There was no smile now. Only the dimple in her chin remained. Monica's face was smooth, olive-dark, gilded by the lampglow. Gunn had no doubt that she meant what she said. He felt a shiver run up his spine.

"You think they might bother you?" he asked.

"Not really. I don't think they have the *cojones*."

Gunn winced at the small obscenity. Monica was clearly an unusual woman.

"I guess not," he said. "How's Debbie?"

"She's a prisoner, Gunn. And obviously she was falling in love with you. I can see why. You're everything she said you were—except dead." The smile broadened, the dimples deepened. "She said you were big, handsome, with gray-blue eyes that looked right through a woman."

"Uh, what else did she tell you?"

Monica laughed, reached for her brandy.

"She didn't have to tell me anymore. Don't worry, I'll keep your secret. Under the circumstances, I might have taken you onto my blanket myself."

Gunn started to sweat. Monica's boldness was unnerving. She was not at all like her brother. She had a coarse-edged refinement that was puzzling. Her hands were delicate, veined, the fingers long and slender. She sipped her brandy and he saw the diamonds on the rings she wore on her left hand.

"You're wondering why Juan and I are so different. Everyone does. He is not really my brother. Yet he is, in a way. I am fond of him. He told you about my husband?"

Gunn nodded.

"Lorenzo Miller was a man's man. Proud, strong. A man of the West, Gunn. He used to drive cattle to my father's hacienda in Texas. He sold horses. At one time he was a Texas Ranger. We met, we fell in love. My father objected. Juan, who made saddles and such for my father, Ramon Viernes Hidalgo Y Montero, helped us to run away one night. He also made sure that my father's men could not track us. Papa would have killed Lorenzo, Lonny, if he had found us."

"You were an only child?"

Monica nodded.

"You gave up a great deal for your husband."

"I gave up centuries of tradition, custom. Lonny and I were happy. He made his way and I loved him even more because he resisted my father even after the money was offered him."

"The money?"

"My father's agents found us, but we had already been married. Papa knew that and wanted to give us a grant of land. Many acres. But Lonny knew that we would be under Papa's thumb if we went back. He chose to earn his own way. And he did very well until we came to Socorro." A bitterness crept into Monica's voice. Gunn sipped his brandy, fascinated by her story.

"What happened here?"

110

"We were actually on our way back to Texas. My father was ailing and he had sent for us. This time we knew it was no trick. Lonny had been doing well as a private detective in San Francisco and later was given work in Colorado and Wyoming. He liked the territories better than the glitter of San Francisco. So did I. He was offered the job as Sheriff of Socorro after he finished up in Wyoming. We came here, bought this small house. The town was quiet and we felt we could leave. But Lonny had found out something through his connections. I never found out what. He asked me to stay here a while longer while he did some checking. The next thing I knew, he was dead. Murdered."

"Not suicide?"

"No!" Monica's eyes flashed and then she quieted down, drew herself up on the chair as if struggling for composure. "No. That was the story around town, but I never believed it. Lonny was shot in the back of the head. With his own pistol. I saw him—saw him afterwards."

"Could he have killed himself?"

"It—it would have been awkward. But I know he didn't. I—I bathed and dressed him before he was buried. Someone had beaten him. With something soft. There were no marks on his face, but his whole body was terribly bruised. There were marks on his neck as if someone had strangled him. He was choked and then shot."

"Have any idea who did it?"

Monica shook her head.

"It could have been anyone. The town was wild.

111

Rough. Lonny had cleaned it up, but there were men who hated him."

"Larrabee?"

"Maybe. Some of the rougher men came back after Lonny was killed and may work for Larrabee. I can't prove anything, of course."

"What about Caleb Barnes? Was he working on that?"

"I—I don't know. He could have been. He was very fond of Lonny. This all happened three years ago. I went to see my father, then came back here and bought the hotel." Gunn's eyebrows went up. "Oh, yes. I own it, but no one knows that, except you and Lorna Starr. I want to find out who killed Lonny. I will stay here until I know."

Gunn let out a breath. He was stunned by Monica's story. It told him much and it told him nothing. There were so many unanswered questions. But Monica, he decided, was a brave woman. And determined. He was about to ask her what she would do if she found out who had killed her husband, but there was a heavy pounding on the door just then. Gunn set the brandy snifter down on the floor and reached for his pistol.

Monica stiffened, her eyes went wide.

"Open up, *puta!* Open up or I'll break this door down!"

Gunn put his finger to his lips. The door shook as the man on the other side rattled the latch.

The man cursed in Spanish. Even though he had spoken English, he had a heavy Mexican accent.

"It's Gordo!" Monica whispered. "And he's drunk!"

The door creaked as a heavy body leaned against it.

"Blow out the lamp," Gunn whispered, and ran to the door. Monica raced to the lamp, blew into the chimney. The lamp went out.

Gunn opened the door.

CHAPTER NINE

A few moments earlier, Gordo sat against the tree swigging on a bottle of whiskey. He kept looking at the house across the street. The man who sat across from him, under the other tree had been goading him for a half an hour.

"You'd like some of that, wouldn't you, Gordo? Had your eye on Monica Miller for some time."

"I could have her any time I wanted."

"Bullshit," cackled Harve Newsome, a man in his forties with a face puffed from strong drink, nearly bald, a game leg. "That woman's uppitier'n any white woman. She'd scratch yore eyes out, bite your balls off before breakfast."

"Hell, no woman could do that," said Gordo, wincing at the thought of being castrated by a woman's teeth. "'Specially no Mexican woman."

Gordo shifted his weight, set the bottle down. He was a huge, powerfully built man whose bulk dwarfed the tree trunk he leaned against. He had strong hands, thick as roots. His arms and shoulders were corded with muscles. Men gave him a wide berth, generally, because he could crush a man in those arms with a single squeeze.

"I dare you to go over there, Gordo, and put the boots to her."

"We got to stay here, Harve."

"Hell, it wouldn't take long. Ain't that what the stud rabbit said to the bunny?" Harve laughed.

"Huh?"

Newsome let out a sigh. Sometimes it was like talking to a kid trying to palaver with Gordo.

"You ain't heard that story? Stud rabbit halts this gal rabbit, asks her for a little. Gal rabbit says she's in a helluva hurry. The buck rabbit says to her: 'Hell, it won't take long, did it?'"

Gordo didn't laugh.

Newsome snorted and took another pull on his bottle. It was turning cold and he shrugged deeper into his sheepskin jacket. That was the trouble with this country. Hotter'n the hinges of hell during the day and colder'n a well-digger's ass at night. He looked over at the house again, itching to start something. It was boring as hell sitting next to the ashes of a burned down house for some stupid reason. That damned Larrabee was contrary as hell at times. But, he paid good. Later on, they'd have to start another fire, though. Just to keep warm.

"Imagine that gal would sure give a man a good ride," said Newsome. "Wonder what she does over there at night. All alone like that."

Gordo looked over at the house. Black eyes buried behind high cheekbones. Glittering like agates. He thought about the woman. Hers was the only house with a lamp glowing behind the shades. The other houses were dark, silent as boxes in a stage office. He

115

wondered why anyone would frame in an adobe. The weather would get to the boards, rot them out. Adobe lasted damned near forever. The woman had fancy ideas. She had come back when no one had expected her to after her man had died. Gordo thought about that. Flexed his fingers.

He could almost feel Lorenzo Miller's throat in his grip again. As if it was yesterday. The slow squeeze, the blood pulsing against his fingers, harder and harder until . . . Miller had taken a long time to die. Which was the way Larrabee had wanted it. Choke him a little, beat on him some more. Choke, then beat. Most men would have started crying and say anything you wanted them to, but not Miller. He had been stubborn. Like a suck-egg mule. Larrabee wanted to know what Miller had on him, but Miller never gave him the satisfaction. He didn't whine. He didn't cry. He just passed out and then came back to for another beating. They used an axe handle on him. Pounded his guts to jelly. And he got to put his hands around the bastard's neck and make his eyes pop out like a frog's. Except the last time he'd pressed too hard and broken the windpipe. Crushed it like a matchbox. Larrabee had been mad as a hornet. So mad he'd taken Miller's pistol and put it to the man's head. And pulled the trigger. Cool as anything. Not a flicker in Larrabee's eyes. Not a muscle twitching. Larrabee had gone up a notch or two in Gordo's book after that. Miller was dying anyway, but to blow out his brains in such a nerveless fashion had been something to see. Only him and Jake had been there with Larrabee. Both had gotten raises on the spot. Jake put the pistol in Miller's hand and left him there with his head on the table just like he'd done it himself.

So, Monica Miller had buried her man and then gone off to Texas. No one ever thought she'd be back. But she had come back and was working at the hotel. Kept her distance from everyone, except for Juan and Corazón Yglesia. Maybe Harve was right. She thought she was better than anyone else in Socorro.

"She's in there, all right," said Newsome. "Probably getting into her nightie right now. You could mosey over there, see if she'd like some. Call me over when you're finished. I don't mind seconds now and then. Not if it's a good chunk like that one."

"She is not so much woman. Probably dried up from not using it for so long."

"Not that one. She probably works on herself ever' night."

Gordo couldn't take that. He considered it an insult if a woman lay with another woman or played with herself. A personal insult. He took it as a slap to his own *machismo*. Any woman who didn't want a man like him between her legs was crazy. Stupid.

Gordo stood up, stepped away from the tree. He unbuttoned his fly. Made water. He sprayed the ashes, listened to the hissing sound of his urine hitting the hot wood.

"You shake it more'n once you're playing with it, Gordo." Newsome chuckled to himself.

Gordo looked across the street again. Idly fingered his manhood. The flesh was warm in his hand.

He thought about Monica Miller. Let his mind roam over her face and neck, her shoulders, breasts. He undressed her, saw the dark thatch between her legs, the graceful smoothness of her legs, the slightly mounded tummy, the belly button like a doodlebug hole in the middle. He wondered how she would look in a delicate nightie, all ready for a man. Ready for a man bold enough to take her.

Gordo put his penis back in his pants, but he didn't button his fly.

"You goin' over there, Gordo?"

"I might," Gordo said. "You keep your mouth shut if I do."

"I ain't no blabbermouth. You just put the boots to her and call me if you need any help." Newsome laughed at himself again.

"She won't want any more when I get finished with her." Gordo threw back his shoulders, hitched his belt. He swayed there next to the smouldering foundation of the Barnes house, staring at the house across the street—a white ghost on a dark street.

Newsome laughed again, slapped his thigh.

Gordo started toward the house. Newsome watched him, envious. Maybe it wouldn't be so boring after all. If Gordo got inside, rutted with that Mexican gal . . .

Gordo reached the porch. Newsome heard his boots hollow on the boards. Heard him pound on the door. Heard the sound of his voice asking to be let in. Newsome started to chuckle. Then, the light went out and he heard the creak of a hinge. The door

118

opening. Gordo inside.

"I'll be a sonofabitch," muttered Newsome to himself. "It was easy. Easy as pie . . ."

* * *

Gunn jerked the door open fast.

Gordo tumbled into the pitch room. The door slammed behind him.

"Eh?" he asked. *"Mujer?"*

Gunn brought both fists down on the back of the Mexican's neck. Pistol in his grip, his hands crunched into hard bone. The butt of the pistol dug into a shoulder. There was the smack of flesh hitting flesh. The heavy-set Mexican dropped like a pole-axed steer. Grunted like a rooting hog.

Gunn saw Monica move out of the corner of his eye. A shadowy wraith gliding across the room.

"Is he . . . ?"

"Stay away," Gunn husked.

Gordo was on his knees, but not out. An ordinary man would have been chewing on floor boards with a blow like that. Eating splinters and rug. But the bull of a Mexican was already rising to his feet. Gunn felt an arm lock around his leg. A powerful hand grasped his calf. Excruciating pain shot through Gunn's leg. It was like being caught in a vise. A tightening, bone-crushing vise.

Gordo's massive shape blotted out the faint light in the room. His hand slid up Gunn's leg, going for the nuts.

Gunn brought the barrel of his Colt down across

the forearm. He aimed his blow by instinct. Something gave way. The grip on his leg loosened. But he felt huge hands reaching for his throat. Smelled hot whiskey breath blowing on his face.

Gunn tried to slide away. A knee came up, rammed into his crotch. Blinding flashes of pain shot through his groin.

"Gunn? What's happening?"

Monica moved behind the divan, suddenly afraid.

Only savage grunts answered her question.

Gordo slammed Gunn hard against the wall. The room shook. Sound reverberated through the walls.

Stars flashed in his head and fingers dug into his shoulders, sought his throat. The pistol fell from Gunn's hand, clattered on the floor.

"Hijo de puta!" snarled Gordo.

Gunn twisted sideways, trying to elude the deadly grip of the Mexican. Fingers closed around his neck. The pressure blotted out all reason. A black shape crawled up the walls of his brain. He had seconds to live if he could not break the Mexican's grip. That long, no more.

Monica knew something was terribly wrong. She saw only the massive dark shape of Gordo, heard the breaths of the struggling men, the thunk of bone against the wall. She knew she had to act fast or Gunn would fall victim to those deadly hands. Gordo's reputation was well-known in Socorro. In a fight, anyone who got near him soon found himself gasping for breath. She dashed around the divan, ran to the door. Snatching up the rifle, she hissed a warning.

"Turn him loose!"

Gunn barely heard her. The black shape in his brain clogged his thoughts. A hard ringing in his ears told him that he was losing consciousness. His breath whistled through his teeth. His eyes bulged in their sockets, while a nerve in his neck twanged like a tautened guitar string oddly out of tune.

Monica swung the rifle butt. Heard it crack against Gordo's head like a club thunking an over-ripe melon.

Gordo grunted and swore with rage.

But his hands relaxed enough so that Gunn could wrench himself free of the strong man's grip.

Gordo whirled on his attacker, lunged at Monica.

A stifled cry issued from her throat.

Gunn lashed out a booted foot, caught Gordo in the kneecap. The burly Mexican staggered and Gunn threw two quick punches into the man's kidneys. Gordo shoved Monica backwards and turned to find Gunn once again.

"You bastard. I will kill you!" Gordo growled.

"Come ahead," said Gunn, backing away.

Gordo's arms were held out at his sides like giant pincers. He stalked the shadowy Gunn on surprisingly quick feet. Gunn shot an overhand right. It landed high on Gordo's forehead. The blow would have brought a normal-sized man to his knees. Gordo shook it off as if tapped by a five-pound sack of flour.

"Be careful!" Monica warned, as she rose to her feet. She had sagged against the front door when Gordo had turned on her. Now, she was frightened.

Bewildered. Terrified of the violence in her home.

Gunn knew that he was in a bad spot.

In the dark, he couldn't see clearly. The shadowy hulk seemed to take up all the space in front of him. Advancing on him like a mountain rising out of a thick fog. A mountain about to crash down on him, crush him like a bug. Gunn shot a hard left straight to the Mexican's midsection. The sound of his fist hitting Gordo's gut was like the smack of a wet towel on a hollow gourd and had about the same effect.

Backing away, Gunn's mind raced. If Gordo closed in on him, he was a goner. Somehow, he had to box the man, confuse him. Dance in and out quick as lightning. And hit him. Hard as hell. Hard enough to hurt him. Hurt him enough and he might have a chance.

But where to hit the Mexican? His fist disappeared inside the big man's stomach like a shot bag in a quicksand bog. Blows bounced off the man's head with all the telling effect of hail on a tin roof. Yet the man had to have a soft spot. Some weakness. He reeked of whiskey, which probably explained why the man hadn't gone down and stayed down. But, he was also strong. Bull-strong, with layers of protective fat under his hide.

Gunn's testicles ached where the Mexican had kneed him.

And there was his answer.

Behind him, Gunn felt a faint breeze. The hallway! If he could back into it, he would have the advantage. Like an animal inside a cave, he could hold the Mexican at bay.

122

By feel, the faint whisper of air on the back of his neck, Gunn backed up to the hallway entrance. Monica was moving somewhere across the room. He couldn't see her, but he heard a crash as a table, or perhaps the footstool, fell over.

"Come on, fat man," Gunn taunted.

With a savage grunt, Gordo waddled after Gunn, head lowered, arms spread wide, curved toward his enemy.

Gunn slipped into the hall, stood his ground.

When the Mexican's fists crunched into the walls of the living room, Gunn was ready. He kicked hard, aiming between the Mexican's legs. The toe of his boot struck something soft, then thudded against bone.

Gordo screamed and doubled over in agony.

Gunn brought a fist up from the floor. He threw his shoulder into the punch and felt a shock as his fist slammed into Gordo's face. Pain shot up his arm clear to the shoulder.

But Gordo fell backward, then rolled onto his side. He groaned, his hands grasping his shattered scrotum. He moaned before Gunn brought a boot down on his head. There was a sickening crunch, the *thwunk* of Gordo's head hitting the wooden flooring.

Then, silence.

In the far corner of the room, a match flared.

Gunn looked up, saw Monica touch a match to a candle.

"Gunn?"

"Yes."

"Are you all right?"

"A little sore here and there. Bring the light over."

The candle flame wavered as Monica threaded her way toward him. She held the brass candle holder by its graceful handle, edged around the divan. She stood over the hulk of Gordo, played the flickering light over the Mexican's face.

Gordo's eyes were closed. Blood oozed out of his mouth. His hands were tucked between his legs. He looked like an oversized baby, sleeping.

"Jesus, he's big," said Gunn.

"They call him Gordo." Monica shuddered. "He could have crushed your head like an egg."

Gunn felt his throat.

"I know. He one of Larrabee's men?"

"Uh huh. One of those across the street."

Gunn walked over, retrieved his pistol. Put it back in its holster.

"Who's the other man?"

"Harvey Newsome. Harve. He probably put Gordo up to this."

"Well, he'll be wondering about this big feller. I don't want a swarm of people in here. You got any rope, something to gag this one with?"

"Yes, in the closet by the back porch."

"Get me enough for two men. It would take a team of mules to haul this man outside. I think we'll just keep them both hogtied for the rest of the night."

Monica disappeared down the hall to get the rope and cloth for gags. Gunn huffed and puffed, dragging the unconscious Gordo to the front door. The man would live, but he was deep under. Gordo sniffled and sputtered, choked on his own blood.

Gunn left him there, opened the front door. Monica had the candle with her, so it was still dark in the front room. He hoped he could imitate Gordo's voice enough to fool the man across the street in the now-vacant lot.

"Harve!"

A moment passed.

"Gordo?"

"*Si*. You want some of this?"

Another pause.

"Hell yeah! Be right there, Gordo."

Gunn swung the door back, left it open just a crack.

He picked up the rifle, stood there, just inside, waiting.

Monica was still in the back. He could hear her opening and closing a door. Light splashed from beyond the kitchen, a dim glow in the dark of the house.

"Gordo? Open up."

Gunn flicked the door open with the toe of his boot.

Harve Newsome stepped inside just as Gunn stepped back a long stride.

"Damn if you didn't do it, Gordo . . . I can't wait . . ."

Gunn swung the rifle by the barrel. The stock *whished* through the air.

The heavy wood crashed into Newsome's face with a stomach-wrenching crunch. *Whup!*

Newsome's eyes rolled into the back of their sockets. His knees buckled and he sagged to the floor.

Gunn bet that he would never know what hit him.

Monica came down the hall, carrying rope and some rags. The candlelight shimmered on her face.

Gunn pulled Newsome out of the doorway, shut the door.

"Only two of them across the street?"

"Y-yes, I think so. That's Harve Newsome. Is he dead?"

"Bad headache. I'll cut rope and you can start tearing those rags up into long strips."

Gunn drew his knife, cut the rope into workable lengths. The knife was a gift, made in Mexico. The legend on the blade was in Spanish. *No me saques sin razon, ni me guardes sin honor.*

"Do not draw me without reason, nor keep me without honor."

He bent Gordo's legs back, tied his feet. He did the same with his arms. Then, he laced the feet and hands together as tight as he could. He did the same with Newsome, but it was easier working with the lighter man. Now he could do the rest of it.

"I'll be back for Newsome," he said, dragging Gordo back through the front door. It was rough going. The Mexican weighed over two hundred pounds and it was all dead weight. He lugged him to the far edge of the lot, shoved him against one of the trees. He returned, and dragged Newsome over to the other tree.

"Good night, boys," he said to no one. "If you get too cold, just holler."

Monica was waiting for him.

She was trembling.

"Gunn," she breathed. "Don't go. And don't sleep

126

in the guest room. I want you with me. In my bed."

"Monica . . ."

"Shh!" she whispered. "Don't argue with a woman who knows what she wants and will pay any price to get it."

"I won't say another word."

CHAPTER TEN

Monica lit the lamp in her bedroom with the candle. She blew out the candle and the scented smoke hung in the air. The aroma of pine lingered as Gunn watched her undress. She seemed oblivious to his presence, as he sat on the edge of the bed, tugging at his boots.

He was still sore. His scrotum felt as if it had been crushed by a herd of wild horses. His shoulders ached. The wound in his skull throbbed with an insistent pain.

But Monica made him forget his hurts.

Her clothes whispered off her body and she stepped out of her skirt and panties like a water nymph, her flesh burnished with the coppery light of the lamp. Gunn slid out of his buckskins, tossed them on the floor at the foot of the bed.

Monica walked to the dressing table, brushed her hair. She was stark naked. He saw that she had dimples in her back, as well. Deep ones just above her hips. Delicately rounded buttocks jutted out as she stooped to see her face in the mirror. Her hair crackled with electricity. Her smooth back gleamed golden in the lampglow.

Gunn felt heat invade his loins. The first stirrings of desire erased the ache in his scrotum.

When she came to him, moments later, he was ready.

He took her into his arms, fell back on the bed.

"You were magnificent tonight," she breathed. *"Muy macho."*

Her hand found his manhood, grasped it tightly as if gripping the stalk of some wild plant.

Gunn felt a surge of pleasure through his loins.

"You're big, too."

He kissed her on the forehead. She threw her head back and leaned into him, her lips seeking his. He pulled her to him, felt her breasts mash against his chest. Her hand stroked his swollen member, forcing hot juices through the slit in the mushroomed crown.

"Do you hurt much?" she asked, breaking the kiss. Her mouth was wet, glistened like a flower wet with rain.

"No. Not much. Not anymore."

Her hand touched his scrotum and he winced.

"I'm sorry," she said. Her hand caressed the sac delicately and the small pain went away.

Monica knew how to treat a man, he decided. She knew much. Her touches told him just how much. He figured he was swollen some, but not injured in any permanent way. The balls would go back to normal in a few hours. Painful at the time, but Gordo's knee hadn't crushed anything essential.

129

"Feel better?" she asked.

"Some better," he admitted.

"Let me kiss it."

He watched as she curled around, put her head between his legs. Her neck bowed as she bent to kiss him. She held his sac up gently in her hand and kissed him lavishly. Soft kisses light as snow tinkling on an aspen leaf. Little nudges against his tender flesh. Then, the peppery flick of her tongue all over the still-swollen sac. Up against the hard base of his cock. Fire shoots up his spine. A spreading warmth in his loins.

Her tongue traced a path up the length of his rigid shaft. Clear to the damp crown. Encircling it with the hot wet tip until he wanted to plunge it between her wet lips. He grabbed her hair, entwining his fingers in its lushness, fingers gently clutching her skull.

She opened her mouth, drew his throbbing cock inside. Tongued the crown with sweeping strokes until he thought he would explode at that very moment. She drew him in deep. Her cheeks hollowed out from the suction. Her head bobbed up and down, sliding over the length of his manhood, her lips squeezing him with a delightful pleasure.

Gunn rubbed the smooth expanse of her back. His hand found a soft breast, kneaded it tenderly. The nipple sprang to life, hardened into a nubbin. The other breast presented itself as Monica slid her body in a different direction. Gunn brought the nipple out of its bed, rubbing its rough face with a single finger

130

until it, too, was hard as an acorn.

Monica suckled him until he had to hold on to keep from spilling his seed. He wrapped an arm around her waist, drew her away from his cock. He brought her head up to his own, kissed her, sliding his tongue inside her mouth. She tasted of salt and lemon, of a dank seashore at full tide. And her hair floated around his face like spiderwebs, imparting a delicious tingle to his skin. Her tongue delved deep into his own mouth, raked his tongue, teased it with flicker-jabs that sent distant spears of pleasure through his groin.

She wallowed atop his body, her loins rubbing against his own. He felt her bristle-haired nest thrust against his manhood, scratch the sensitive skin as it slid up and down. He felt her heat, the wetness as her pussy-lips parted. Felt the slick inner lining of the labiae oiling his member, caressing it with silken pleasure. Her nipples razed his chest like rubbery thumbs and as her arms locked around his neck, the breasts flattened into warm sponges gently sliding over his naked flesh.

"I want you, Gunn," she husked, her voice a whisper in his ear. "I want you inside me as deep as you can go."

He rolled her over on her back, gazed down at her dark eyes lambent in the glow of the lamp.

He was glad she had left the lamp on so that he could see her at that moment. Her breasts were soft mounds rising from her chest. Her flat belly quivered as he rose above her. Her black hair glistened like moonlight on a crow's wing. Her eyes glittered with desire.

She spread her legs and he looked down at the shadowed thatch between them. The blunt cliff her bones made so that her womanhood jutted upward to receive him. He slid into her, lowering his loins, the curved scimitar of his shaft poised for the plunge through her portals. Monica raised her hips, thrust her sex-cleft upward for the impalement.

His manhood cleaved into her, parting the lips of her sex and sinking into steaming folds of soft flesh.

Monica quivered as he entered her. Shuddered with a deep ripple of pleasure. She felt him burrow deep, touch all the tingling places. The first touch was like a faint flow of electricity. Deeply satisfying. As if someone had plucked a melodious chord somewhere in the magic part of her brain where dreams lay fallow. As he stroked her, the chord deepened, the music, an indefinable substance, surged up in a thrilling crescendo. She bucked as he touched her love-button, and loosed the first orgasm.

"Ah, Gunn," she breathed. "You're beautiful. Ummmm. You're touching everything. *Everything.*"

He rammed deep then, held onto her twisting, writhing body. Her kisses peppered his face and neck. Her hands groped at his flesh, kneading the muscles, squeezing the cords underneath the skin. Her loins moved in rhythm with his own, impaling herself on his throbbing cock.

"I've never been so excited in my life," she said, after the third orgasm. "Every time you stroke me, I melt inside."

"A pleasure, Monica." His voice was low, throaty.

"Yes, Gunn. A pleasure."

Gunn plumbed her slow, then, knowing she was his, that he could satisfy her. Monica was a warm, loving woman, fiery and tender at the same time. She was a lovely creature, beautiful in the glow of the lamp which flickered warmly in the shadow-filled room. Her flesh flowed with a coppery light. Her eyes glittered like basking coals, flashing her pleasure with each of his thrusts, closing in the throes of each climax.

Monica felt the jolting pops on every slow stroke now. Gushing freshets of pleasure oozed through her loins every time Gunn's spear slid over the tuberous trigger that was the wellspring of her excitement. She looked up into Gunn's pewter eyes and felt the melting sensation as if molten fire were filling her crevice. His broad shoulders, his massive chest, glistened bronze, his body oiled with the sweat of his passion. His dark hair fell boyishly over his forehead as he returned her look.

Memories of her Lonny welled up in her mind, faded. Lorenzo had been a good strong man, but he was not the lover that Gunn was. She felt guilty even comparing the two men. Yet she had known no man since Lorenzo's death. Nor had she wanted one. But seeing Gunn tonight, his strength, his victory over the two outlaws, had stirred up memories of her late husband. The similarities between Lonny and Gunn were not visible to the naked eye. Rather, she saw Gunn's courage and his essential goodness as similar to the same qualities her husband had possessed. Gunn had done more than stir memories of Lonny,

133

however. He had kindled banked fires, sparked hidden pockets of flame, forcing them to flare up and light shadowy corners of her mind, her being.

She bucked with a sudden and unexpected orgasm as Gunn plunged deep. She held onto him until the awesome spasms had passed. Gunn stayed his movements until her shudders subsided, then withdrew his organ slowly. Monica bucked again. Held on. Her moans filled the silence in the room. Moans of pleasure. Moans of yearning long held back, suppressed.

"Yes, yes," she breathed. "Oh, it's good. So damned good."

Gunn suckled her breasts, taking each in turn. Took the nipples in his mouth, worried them to a button hardness. He did this in between strokings, resting while Monica caught her breath. She writhed in ecstasy, smeared his neck with hot kisses.

"I want to get on top," she said, later. "Would you care?"

"No."

Monica's eyes danced with the light of eagerness.

Gunn slid from her body, rolled over on his back. Monica scrooched up, straddling him. She raised herself above his swollen stalk, lowered her buttocks. Gunn held onto them, guiding her down. He speared her perfectly and she slid onto his shaft. She arched her back, gazed up at the ceiling as Gunn's cock sank home.

"Oh, yes," she sighed. "Oh, that feels good. You don't know . . ."

He watched her, fascinated. She seemed locked in

a world of her own as she rose and fell on his shaft. Her arms were straight, hands pushing off his waist, her back slightly arched, her legs spread wide. She bobbed up and down, first fast, then slow, gliding her sheath over his cock so that it made contact with her pleasure-trigger at all times. Her breasts were turned up pertly. Her skin shone with perspiration, a copper-gold in the dancing light from the lamp.

Monica seemed transported. She rose and fell faster and faster. Her fingers clutched at Gunn's flesh as she shivered in orgasmic convulsions. She cried out, moaned, sobbed and hung there, once, as a bone-rattling orgasm ripped through her body. She fell to one side, exhausted. Rolled over on her back.

"Take me again," she husked.

Gunn mounted her and thrust deep.

"Faster," she said.

Gunn, his body oiled with sweat, bucked into her, ramming deep, stroking faster than before.

Monica screamed.

Screamed with joy, with pleasure. She was soaked inside, her honeypot boiling and bubbling.

"Don't stop. Not now, Gunn. I—I've never been pleasured so much by any man!"

It was too late to slow down or stop. Gunn felt his own juices leap to a boiling point. Pleasure was now a single line of current running through his body, spreading out, through the nerves like the tendrils on a tree leafing out in springtime. Pleasure was warmth and wetness, flashing lights in his brain, tingles up and down his spine. And Monica like a thrashing animal beneath him, moaning and sighing, undulating with unleashed energy.

"Now!" she screamed, clutching him with steel fingers, pulling his hips downward, locking his loins to hers. "Now, Gunn, now!"

He let it go. The rush of seed, the blinding flash of pleasure. The exquisite pain/pleasure of the moment when his sperm shot, his seminal vesicle emptied. The sweet sadness of release as his cock spilled its milky secretion, jetting deep into Monica's womb.

Monica smothered Gunn's face with kisses, clasped him tightly to her breasts until the final shudder.

Sated, Gunn rolled from her body. The wick burned low and Monica leaned over, extinguished the flame.

The room was plunged into darkness except for the faint light of stars and moon that leaked in through the curtains.

"Thank you, Gunn," whispered Monica. Her hand grazed his thigh. Fingers spanned his leg. "It's been a long time. Almost three years."

"You shouldn't deprive yourself, Monica. You're a mighty comely woman, and a loving one to boot."

She sighed deeply. Her hand found him in the dark, caressed his limp flesh.

"I have never found a man to fill Lorenzo's boots."

"Each man is different. Each person."

"I know. No one could ever replace Lonny. But there are not many men who could match up to him, either. You were married before?"

"Yes."

"What happened?"

"She died."

"I'm sorry."

"I'm sorry for you, too."

"I guess life wasn't meant to be smooth or easy."

"No. Most of the time we make it harder than it's supposed to be."

Their talk died down. Gunn took her in his arms, felt her tremble. She fell asleep. Gunn listened to her breathing until his own eyes grew heavy. He slept, the woman locked in his arms and he did not think about the morrow and the glare of reality. He thought only of the island he was on now and the woman who slept so close they were almost one.

* * *

Gunn sipped the strong coffee, peered through the front window. Dawn was just streaking the sky, splaying it with cream along the eastern horizon. His face felt new, soft, where he had shaved with Lorenzo's straight razor. Across the street, he saw the remains of the fire: the massive wood stove still fuming in what must have been the kitchen, the smouldering divan, some smoking chairs, a collapsed wardrobe, tatters of clothing, kitchen utensils, boots, shoes. An adobe chimney stood like a stark sentinal over the ruins. Beyond, two shapes lay next to the trees. Gordo and Harve.

"Where did the lumber come from for your house and Caleb's?" Gunn asked. He realized now that

Barnes' house had been a wood frame. It must have gone up like dry tinder.

Monica was just coming into the front room, coffee cup in hand. The aroma filled the house. A fire crackled in the fireplace, dispelling the chill. She had been up before dawn, cooked breakfast, brought in water for Gunn to shave and bathe with before she served him fatback, hot cakes, biscuits and blueberry syrup.

"A boat ran aground here one summer. Caleb and Lorenzo bought the lumber from it. Caleb had his house built and Lorenzo framed this adobe in for better insulation and appearance. Why?"

"Just curious. This is adobe country. Not much lumber. Have to haul timbers a long ways."

"There was enough lumber on the boat to go around. Then Larrabee and Lorna Starr had more brought in for the false fronts on the main street. This used to be a town that wanted to be respectable."

"What happened?"

Monica stood by Gunn, looking out the window. She put an arm in his.

"Greed. Fear. The only reason Socorro's still alive is that there's so much empty space out there between El Paso and Santa Fe. People stop here, spend money. But the town doesn't grow anymore. It's gaining a bad reputation. Lorna would like to change all that. Larrabee doesn't give a damn. He'll suck it dry and move on."

"Odd he hasn't already," Gunn mused.

"Yes, it is, isn't it?"

"Any law here?"

138

Monica looked away sadly.

"Not since Lonny was killed. The town tried to organize, but Larrabee's men outvoted any others. Larrabee's the law here."

Gunn finished his coffee.

"I'm going on into town," he said. "I don't want to get you in trouble on my account. Soon as Larrabee's men find those two hogtied over there, he'll come lookin' for me."

"You don't have to go," she said, looking into Gunn's blue-gray eyes. "I'm not afraid of Larrabee."

"I'll be back tonight. I want to poke through those ashes over there. Caleb left something behind. It might not be burned up."

Even as he spoke, two wagons rumbled up to the ruins of Caleb's house. Gunn saw the breath of the men on the chill morning air. The horses, too, blew steamy plumes through their nostrils. The sound of gruff voices drifted across the street.

"Looks as if someone beat you to it," Monica said, going back to the window, pulling the curtain aside.

Gunn frowned.

The drovers dismounted, ran to the struggling hulks next to the trees. Gunn heard men cursing. The drovers stooped to untie Harve and Gordo. There was more loud talking, gesturing. No one pointed toward the house, however. Gunn figured that Gordo and Harve wouldn't want to tell the truth just yet. It might cost them their jobs. Still, he saw Gordo look toward Monica's house a couple of times. He could almost feel the anger and hatred travel across the street.

139

While they were looking, there was a loud knocking at the back door.

Gunn whirled, but Monica put a hand on his arm.

"It's for me. The hotel sends an escort over every morning. Wait here. I'll only be a minute. More coffee?"

Gunn shook his head.

He watched the four men across the street. They unloaded shovels from the wagons, began sifting through the smoking debris. Gordo and Harve carried junk to the wagons while the drovers shoveled through the ashes.

Gunn heard a man speaking in rapid Spanish to Monica. He couldn't make out the words. Monica's voice rose and fell, the words muffled.

He was glad that Gordo wasn't bent on revenge this early in the morning. The man still shot murderous glances in his direction, but Gunn stayed well back of the window. Finally, he walked over and stood in front of the fire. The logs crackled and the flames were soon too hot to stand. It was time to leave. He started toward the hall when Monica entered the room.

Her face was chalk-white.

"Bad news?" he asked.

Monica nodded.

"It's Debbie Barnes. I have to go there right away."

Gunn's scalp prickled.

"Did Larrabee . . ."

Monica shook her head.

"She's miscarrying. A midwife's been called. I

140

must go to her, see if I can help. Gunn, I'm scared . . ."

He held her, felt her shake against him.

"Of Larrabee?"

"No, not him. Not now. It's Debbie . . . she might die . . ."

CHAPTER ELEVEN

Debbie bit down hard on the piece of towel in her teeth.

Tears rolled down her face. Her body twisted and writhed in agony.

Larrabee's man, a nervous thin Mexican named Jaime Nieves, looked into the room. He stood in the hall, a tic working under his left eye, wondering if he should leave his post and tell Larrabee what was going on. The woman had started screaming early that morning and several guests in the hotel had been awakened. One of them had protested so much he'd had to open the door.

What he had seen had been most terrible.

There was blood all over the bed and the girl was screaming like a tortured animal.

Someone had gone for the midwife, Julieta Garcia. People had gotten angry with him for letting the girl suffer like that. But it wasn't his fault. He had been told to guard the girl and let no one in or out. Now he wondered if he had done right letting someone bring in the midwife. But the screaming had gone on until he had gotten a towel from the rack and given it to the girl.

"Bite on this," he had said, and the girl had nearly bitten his hand off.

But the screaming had stopped. Now, the girl was sweating gallons of water and the veins in her face and neck looked as if they would burst. Jaime did not understand what was wrong, but if Julieta was coming it must have something to do with female troubles. The blood, lots of blood, was mixed with water and yellowish matter that made a man sick to look at it.

The people stood in the hallway, glaring at him. But they didn't come near because Jaime had told them to stay away.

"I will shoot anyone who goes in that room," he told them. So, they muttered among themselves and gave him dirty looks.

There was a commotion on the stairs.

Julieta was coming, barking orders to a man who worked in the hotel. She swept Jaime aside and swooped into the room. She carried a heavy black bag, which she set on the floor next to the bed.

"Agua, traigame mucho agua caliente," she said to him.

Jaime blinked. She expected him to bring hot water? He could not do that. For sure, Larrabee would have him whipped if he left his post.

"No puedo salir," he said. *"Que pas con la mujer?"*

Julieta's answer was to slam the door in his face so that he could not see what was going on. Confused, Jaime yelled at a woman down the hall.

"Get some hot water, bring it fast," he said in Spanish. The woman disappeared and Jaime

143

began sweating.

A few minutes later, Julieta opened the door.

Jaime blinked at her.

"Step aside," she said, "or I'll kick your eggs up in your belly." Jaime took a step backward. "The woman is miscarrying. Send someone to fetch the *Señora,* Monica Miller. I need help."

Jaime stood there, frozen.

"Move!"

Jaime looked in the room, saw that the girl was stark naked with a towel stuffed between her legs. His knees turned to jelly and he started yelling for someone to go after Monica Miller. He could see that Debbie Barnes was not going to go anywhere. One of the men who worked in the hotel, Pepito Salazar, said he was going to fetch her anyway and would deliver the message. Relieved, Jaime went back to his post. He was shaking visibly and his dark skin had paled at least two shades lighter.

Julieta, a dowdy, heavy-set woman in her forties, snorted at him and went back inside the room. She began speaking to him without ever looking at his face.

"You guard the door? Guard the door, but don't let anyone in but the *Señora* and the hot water when it comes. I will need lots of hot water and some more lamps. Help me to pull the bureau over by the bed. And set the lamps on the bureau so that the light will reflect on the bed. This girl is dying and it's all your fault, you worm!"

Confused, Jaime barked orders to those in the hall. He went inside and helped Julieta move the bureau over by the bed. The mirror was tilted to

Julieta's satisfaction. People brought lamps and Jaime saw to it that they were set in front of the mirror.

Light blazed down on the bed. On the naked body of the girl.

The hot water arrived.

"More hot water," Jaime ordered, pleased that he was doing something constructive at last. He did not want the girl to die. Larrabee might beat him for that, too. He thought of sending someone to wake up Larrabee, but reconsidered it. He did not like to be awakened early in the morning. He stayed up late at the Hog & Keg every night and was rarely seen before noon.

"Now, now, *chiquita,*" clucked Julieta, "just lie still. Bite on the towel. It won't hurt much longer. I'm going to take good care of you."

Debbie groaned. Her eyes went wide in stark terror. Sweat beaded up on her forehead. Julieta wiped her brow with a cloth, then began laying out items in her black bag. She lay these on the window-sill next to the bed and on a bedside table.

There were instruments and medicaments, syringes and tourniquets. There were a thermometer and stethoscope, bandages and strings. Julieta laid them all out neatly and then turned to Jaime.

"Close the door. Let only the woman with more hot water and the *Señora* in the room." This she said in English. In Spanish, she added, "and send some-one to bring *El Gallo.*"

Jaime blanched.

There was no priest in Socorro. There was only the medicine man they called *El Gallo.*

145

He closed the door, sure now that the girl would die.

* * *

Gunn left with Monica out the back door of her house.

But he did not go with her to the hotel.

The Mexican who waited for Monica, Pepito Salazar, said that it would be a very bad time for him to accompany the *Señora* to the hotel.

"Jaime is very nervous and he might shoot you," he told Gunn.

"I'll be there later," Gunn told Monica. "Give things a chance to settle down."

"It might be best," said Monica. "The midwife is very capable. If she sent for me it means that she thinks we can handle it. I won't worry until she sends for the medicine man, *El Gallo.*"

"Huh?"

"We do not have a priest in Socorro. Whenever someone is close to dying, Julieta sends for *El Gallo.* She did not do this, Pepito, did she?"

"No. She sent only for you, I think."

"We have no doctor here, either," said Monica. "But we must hurry. If you come to the hotel, come in the back way. I will leave a message at the desk if it is safe to come upstairs. Or tell you where to meet me."

Gunn tipped his hat, watched her and Pepito run toward the hotel. She had given him a quick layout of the town so that he would not get lost. He walked slowly around the edge of the house to check on the

146

men across the street. He made sure they didn't see him. He saw the way they were working and figured he had at least two hours before they got serious. The men were cursing the early morning hour, the cold, the work itself and, without naming him, Larrabee. The man who gave the orders.

Let them do the hard work. Caleb had said that he put the journal under the kitchen stove. The stove was still there. If he'd put the journal under the floor then it was all gone. Up in smoke. If he'd buried it, then the journal might have survived the fire. The worst thing he could do now was to show any interest in the Caleb house. That would alert Larrabee that something important was there. No, let them worry over the ashes, the debris. If they found anything it would be blind luck. The way they were working told him a great deal.

All of the junk was going in one wagon. The partially burned books from the front room were going in the other. The ashes were being piled up on one side of the house's rock foundation. So, Larrabee had probably told them to separate books and papers from everything else, load them in one wagon. The rest was junk. It was certain that he hadn't told the men what he was looking for specifically.

The books hadn't burned through completely, but they were badly charred. For a moment Gunn considered that Caleb might have been mistaken, that he had left the journal out in another room. But there was no way of knowing for sure. For now, he'd have to trust his own instincts.

He crept back around to the rear of Monica's

147

house and hitched his gunbelt up a notch. He squared his hat and set off for Main Street. He had some checking to do before he went to the hotel and found out about Debbie. He was glad that it was early and the town was still half asleep.

The street was quiet, empty.

He saw a horse or two, a small buggy in front of the Rio Grande Hotel. The hotel was midway up the street, on his left. The Hog & Keg was a few doors down, on the right. Beyond that, on the left, was the Rio Queen. There were a number of smaller cantinas, a mercantile store, barber shop, freight office, in between.

Gunn strode toward the Livery Stable at the end of the street, set back from the butcher shop on the corner. Gunn took a good look at the stores on the street and saw the character of the town in one sweeping glance. Slabs of sod piled on top of one another like bricks had been used to put up most of the buildings in Socorro. They were roofed over with more of the same material supported, he knew, by pole rafters cut from some distant slope. Most of the buildings now had false fronts, those oddities of brashness that served as billboards and deceits—proclaiming a better town only to those who didn't look too close.

Neal's Butcher Shop, said the printing on the false front of the corner building. Beyond, Neal's Stable & Livery, its corrals and pens set close to the river so that the water didn't have to be hauled very far. Gunn smelled it before he stepped off the wooden sidewalk. Smelled the dank aroma of dried blood from the butcher shop, the mealy scent of wet saw-dust.

The doors to the livery were closed, but not locked. Gunn slipped the latch string and the wide doors opened on creaking hinges.

A horse nickered from inside.

Sunlight streamed through the opening. A column of light danced with motes of tiny dust particles.

The smell of hay and grain, wet dung and acrid urine. The horse quieted and there was an eerie silence in the stable. The smell of leather and wood, of animal hides. The sound of a horse biting down on dried corn, oats. A hoof pawing through damp straw. The smell of horse sweat and dead coals in the forge. The murmur of flies buzzing lazily in the chill of the barn, awakened by the creeping warmth of the sunlight streaming through the half-open door.

Gunn stepped down the line of stalls, looking into each one, his eyes adjusting to the light. Horses gazed at him over nonchalant shoulders, went back to their feeding. Someone had pitched hay to them; had rattled grain into their feed bins from tin scoops. Brushes and currycombs hung from nails. Halters and bridles.

"Anybody here?" Gunn called. His voice echoed hollow in the gloom of the livery.

He looked up to the rafters, beyond, to the loft. A rat scurried along a board, blinking, twitching its whiskers from a crinkling nose.

Silence.

Gunn walked along, checking each stall.

He stopped at one of them, smiled.

"Howdy, Duke boy," he said quietly.

The horse swung its head back, looked at Gunn. Switched his dark tail over a dun rump. Cocked a rear foot as if to kick, stood hip-shot, switching its tail as the flies boiled up from the dried dung. The Rocking Z brand barely showed, but it was there.

"Go ahead, boy. Eat."

At least, Gunn thought, someone was feeding his horse. Duke, as if understanding the human words, lowered his head back to the trough. No grain, but hay enough to fill his belly.

Gunn walked on to the end of the line of stalls. He made note of the various horses, their brands. All were unfamiliar to him. There were six horses in the livery, room for a dozen. At the other end of the barn, he looked at the saddles hung from the walls, resting on wooden horses. There was his own, the rifle out of its sheath, the saddlebags gone. He cursed silently. He had three hundred dollars concealed in the bottom of a coffee tin. Besides the few dollars in his pocket, the thirty in his pistol, that was all the money he had with him. The rest was in various banks. He could get by for a month or so on what he had with him, but he'd surely need the money in the coffee tin before he reached a town with a telegraph.

He slapped the seat of the saddle, startling the horses. It was a Denver saddle, weighed a good forty pounds. A hell of a chunk of leather and he had worn it to a fine sheen over many miles. For a moment he considered slapping it on Duke's back and just riding on, taking his losses and going on to El Paso for a good week-long drunk. That would be the easy way out. He wouldn't have to worry about Debbie, her dead father, or Monica's dimples or Larrabee or Harve or Gordo. It would be so easy to let the troubles stay in Socorro, put some miles under him and lose about a hundred pounds of misery off his back. He touched the crease in his skull, winced at the tenderness of the wound. A bullet from an unknown rifle had almost put him away for keeps. Did he need that? Who would care? Who would miss him?

No one.

Not a soul.

Gunn took in a breath and knew he couldn't even consider leaving. Not now. He had made a promise. Even if no one knew about that promise, it wouldn't make any difference. He had made it. He knew. And if a man wasn't good for his promise, he wasn't good for anything.

Besides, there was a mystery to solve.

What had Caleb Barnes found out about Larrabee? Why had Larrabee had second thoughts and sent men after the wagon to make sure Barnes was taken care of one way or the other? Why had he burned Caleb's house down to the ground and now had men searching through the ashes for Caleb's journal?

If he, Gunn, didn't call Larrabee to accounts, who would?

The answer was easy.

No one.

Not a damned soul.

He let his breath out and knew he would stay. See it out to the end. Some bastard had shot him, left him for dead and taken away his horse and saddle. That was reason enough for a showdown without all the other reasons. Someone had to be brought up short for all that had happened. Some faces had to be rubbed in the dirt for him to feel better about Caleb, Debbie and the nick in his skull.

A sound distracted Gunn and he turned away from the saddle.

A shadow stretched out across the straw-strewn floor of the livery.

"Hold it right there, mister," said a voice.

The man's face was in shadow, the morning sun behind his head. He had come in through the front, making little sound. Gunn saw the barrels of the shotgun, though. Leveled at his gut.

"You the livery man?" Gunn asked. He tried to think of the name on the front. "Neal?"

"I don't know you," said the voice.

"Name's Gunn."

"Still don't mean nothin' to me. Step out where I can see you good. Keep your hands out away from you."

Gunn did as he was told.

Thirty paces away the man stood, his face still in shadow, hat brim pulled low.

"You don't need that Greener," Gunn said. "I'm not a thief."

"What're you doin' in here?"

"Came to see my horse, ask a few questions."

"You ain't got no horse in here, mister."

"The dun, with the Rocking Z brand on its hip. This here's my saddle, minus the Winchester and saddlebags."

"That so?"

"I say it's so. Lost him yesterday, down the Rio."

"You got papers to prove it?"

"I have." Gunn's stomach sank, but he knew he had to say it anyway. Funny as it would sound and look right then. "In my saddlebags."

The man with the double-barreled shotgun chuckled. It was not a humorous sound at all.

"I got a bunch of confederate money up to the 'dobe, too, mister, but that don't make it any better'n your claim. Drop your gunbelt."

Gunn hesitated.

If he did what the man asked, he'd be in a worse fix than now. Whoever had taken his horse wouldn't just give it up. No, this jasper would turn him over to Larrabee and that would be the last anyone would hear of him. He'd still wind up in the river. Like the halfbreed. Just a day later.

"Well? I'm waitin' and you're makin' me mighty nervous, mister."

"I can't drop my gunbelt. Now, I don't know whose side you're on, feller, but I told you the truth. My horse came in here, I figure, with at least two men. Jake Early and Gus Whitcomb. Maybe another man rode the dun in, but that would make for an extra horse. If you're Neal and you put 'em up, then you know they didn't ride out of here with that dun. Now where in hell do you suppose they made a buy like that all of a sudden?"

The shotgun barrel wavered and Gunn knew he had made at least one point.

The man brought up a hand, wiped it across his mouth.

"You step up close where I can see you," said the man, finally. "No tricks. Not one."

Gunn walked slowly toward the man with the shotgun. He kept his hands in plain sight, smiled.

"That's close enough."

"You Neal?"

"I'm Neal. Saw you skulkin' around here. Now you say Jake took your horse. How'd that come about?"

So now Gunn knew who had ridden Duke in to Socorro. Jake Early.

Gunn told him in a few spare words about the events of yesterday and the day before. He laid it out while staring into the twin barrels of the shotgun. If ever he needed a friend, he knew, it was now.

"That's one hell of a story, Gunn."

"It's true. I walked in here last night. Came straight over here this morning to see if Duke was here."

"Horse know its name?"

"He might. Bought him up the line a ways, but he's carried the handle long before I got his papers."

"Let out his name. Don't turn around, just call it out."

There were six horses in the stalls. Any one of them might respond to a man's voice. A lot of the time it was the tone of a man's voice that caught an animal's attention. He didn't know how well Duke knew his name. Or whether he did at all. Maybe it was only the tone of voice he heard and responded to, not the name itself.

Sweat broke out on Gunn's forehead.

"Duke, boy," he called, just loud enough for the

horse to hear. "Come on Duke!"

Gunn hoped he had pitched his voice right. He used the tone he always did when he was ready to saddle up. He turned, looked toward Duke's stall.

There was a flash of mane. An answering whinney. Duke shifted his position, trotted to the stall's gate. He shook his head, looked at Gunn. Snorted, nodded his head.

Gunn grinned wide.

"Good boy," he said.

CHAPTER TWELVE

El Gallo sat in a corner of the room, his medicine pouch open. A piece of tanned hide lay on the floor in front of him, daubed with kernels of dried corn arranged in a pattern. There were other objects on the hide, as well. Bits of colored string, some with beads, some bare; tufts of stiff hair from squirrel and goat and deer; a seashell; a chunk of polished quartz; dried beans; a clay vial of dried human blood; bear's teeth on a leather thong; various birds' feathers, including hawk and roadrunner. His lips moved, but only a low moan issued from his chest. His eyes opened and closed as he rocked back and forth. He picked up each object, chanting silently to himself, then put it back down to go to another.

Monica bent over the bed. She stood opposite Julieta, who was pushing gently on Debbie's stomach.

Debbie was awake, feverish. Monica dabbed at her face and forehead every so often while Julieta pushed on her belly. Debbie's wrists and ankles were tied securely to the bedposts.

"Is it coming?" Monica asked, in a breathless voice.

"The contractions are starting."

Moments before, Julieta had given ergot to Debbie. Debbie was still biting on the gag in her mouth.

"You've got to push hard, Debbie," Monica said. "Push harder."

Debbie's stomach contracted. Ripples under the flesh. She choked, turned her head to one side as if to vomit. Her hands opened and closed into fists. Her toes curled and straightened with the strain.

The room smelled of carbolic acid, raw alcohol, ointments and salves, lye soap and a dozen other unidentifiable aromas. The lamps burned brightly on the bureau, reflecting brilliance on the patient's abdomen and lower extremities. Monica and Julieta, the midwife, had been working together in silence for the past ten minutes. The strain showed on Monica's face, but Julieta showed no visible sign of emotion. Her hair was held in place by a bandanna and her features set in a grim cast.

"She can't bear much more pain," said Monica.

"If it doesn't come soon, I will have to go inside," said Julieta, pushing down on Debbie's abdomen.

"Is there anything I can do?"

"Pray, *Señora.*"

Monica had been doing that ever since she came into the room. Debbie's complexion horrified her. Chalk white, then dark, her face seemed to be permanently contorted by pain. Julieta had cleaned up most of the blood, shaved her pubic hairs, swabbed the vagina with disinfectant, by the time Monica had arrived. She had also tied the young woman to the bed to prevent her from moving too much or falling off the bed.

The arrival of the medicine man, *El Gallo*, had frightened Monica. He was a fearsome man, a Yaqui, with straight silver-gray hair, deep-sunk eyes, a hawk nose and wrinkled face. He had said some incantations over Debbie and then retreated to a corner of the room after talking to Julieta in a tongue Monica didn't understand. Now, his muttering droned on, punctuated by Debbie's gasps. Now, he shook a gourd rattle, his voice rising and falling as he spoke an ancient language.

Outside the door, Monica knew, Jaime waited. He was nervous and apprehensive. She had issued orders for the hall to be cleared, people to stay away. She left a message at the front desk for Gunn. She didn't want him coming up to Debbie's room. Jaime might draw on him and the last thing they needed was a killing or a wounded man.

Debbie spit out the gag.

"I can't stand it anymore!" she shrieked.

"Hush, child," said Julieta. "It won't be much longer."

But Julieta's eyes looked into Monica's and were cloudy with fear.

"Do you want some spirits?" Monica asked.

Debbie shook her head. Her face was chalk-white, drenched with sweat. Her abdomen contracted just then and she started to double over. Her eyes closed and fresh sweat broke out on her forehead, as the bonds held her straight.

158

Monica wiped the sweat from Debbie's face, saw her muscles twitch in pain as another convulsion, stronger than any others, rippled through her stomach and loins.

"It's coming, I think," said Julieta.

* * *

Neal O'Malley lowered the shotgun, stretched out his hand.

Gunn walked over, shook it.

Neal was in his early thirties, married, with two children. Up close, Gunn saw that he had red hair, blue eyes, and was built solidly, with muscular arms, short bowed legs. He explained to Gunn that the livery and butcher shop were a family operation. He took care of the horses and other stock, sheep and cattle, mostly, occasionally goats, that inhabited the livery and corrals. His father, Neal, Sr., was the butcher.

"We don't hold much with Larrabee's crowd," he told Gunn, "but he pays his bills and buys his beef and mutton from us."

"Where can I find Jake Early?" Gunn asked, feeling that he had made a friend.

"Well, now, you aim to mix it up with Jake?"

"I'd like to get my warbags back."

"Yeah? Easier said'n done."

"I'll try to do it real polite," Gunn said with a grin.

"Early don't know polite, but you'll likely find him at the Hog & Keg. He fits his name when it comes to drinkin' hard liquor. He stays at a shack t'other end of town, but he opens the saloon."

"I'm obliged, Neal."

"No need for thanks. You won't find Jake by himself. He and Whitcomb are thick, and likely Nate Crumb will be there too. They'll have a healthy shot and breakfast, then sit down to cards until Larrabee stirs around noon."

"Those the three that came in yesterday with the girl?"

"I didn't see the girl. Heard about her at the Rio Queen last night. Larrabee put her up at the hotel, after Lorna kicked up a ruckus."

"Did you know Caleb Barnes?"

Neal lowered his head. Kicked at a tuft of straw.

"I knew him. He dead, like they say?"

"Yes. Buried along the river."

"Hell of a note. You're going up against some hard men, Gunn. We try to keep our noses clean here, but it's gettin' mighty messy."

"Where did Larrabee come from?"

Neal shrugged.

"Nobody knows. We've been here most ten years. Larrabee didn't say much when he first come. Then about three years ago, he started taking over the town. Quietlike at first, then he started pushing his way around. Been here about four, five years, I reckon. Caleb asked me about him too."

"And . . . ?"

"I thought about it a lot. When Larrabee first came here he was like a man lookin' over his shoulder. Then, after a year or so, he came out of the bushes. Built up his place, bought some property. Seemed to have money. Don't know where he got it."

Gunn let it go. Neal was a help, but he had nothing

160

solid to go on. There was some mystery concerning Larrabee, but that didn't mean much in itself. All men had pasts. The West was full of men with unsavory histories, but many of them hid their pasts only because they wished to make fresh starts. Evidently Caleb, perhaps Lorenzo Miller, as well, had done some digging into Larrabee's previous life and now both men were dead. One death could be traced back to Larrabee, Caleb's. But Miller's murder had never been solved. Socorro held those secrets and more. And such secrets had a way of coming out when least expected.

"I'll see to it that proof of ownership is established, Neal," Gunn said. "On the dun horse there."

"No need. If you come walking back in here with those saddlebags, I'll take it for granted."

Neal grinned at Gunn and walked outside with him.

Gunn saw that the sun had topped the buildings.

"Another hot one," he said.

"Watch it don't get too hot, Gunn."

Neal saluted, then turned toward a house back of the butcher shop. Gunn saw a pretty woman come out on the porch and shake out a feather duster. He tipped his hat and walked up the street toward the Hog & Keg. A few minutes before, he had seen a man cross the street and head down the street toward Caleb's place. The man had looked at him pretty closely. But Gunn had never seen him before.

* * *

Gordo worked only long enough to get the kinks out of his muscles. The night chill and the immobility had made him stiff. Gordo didn't like to feel that way. He was a man proud of his strength. Since he was a boy he had worked on his muscles, tuned them to a fine hardness. He associated bulging muscularity with masculinity. He liked to show off his arm muscles to admiring girls. He liked to intimidate men with his size, the power in his shoulders and legs and fists.

But this morning he was conscious of having been taken down a notch. The men who had come with the wagons were giving him a wide berth. That was because Gordo had warned them to keep their mouths shut. If they told anyone about him and Harve, he would crack their heads open like melons.

When the wagons were loaded, a man named Blaine Stewart came to relieve Harve and Gordo.

"You boys have a good night?"

"Good enough. You takin' over?" asked Harve. Blaine rubbed sleep out of his eyes.

"Yair. Larrabee says one man can handle it during the day." Stewart hefted his rifle as if to demonstrate that this was all he needed to watch over the property. The fires were all dead now and only ash dust hung in the still morning air.

"Well, we didn't find nothin'," said Harve.

"Didn't think you would. Say, saw a stranger in town."

"Where was this stranger?" asked Gordo, a glimmer of animal cunning in his eyes.

"Over to the livery. Talkin' to young Neal. Just saw him."

"What does he look like?"

"Tall. Wide shoulders. Wearin' buckskins. Never

saw him around before. Might still be there. Neal seemed mighty friendly to him. Couldn't see his face."

"That's him," said Gordo to Harve. "Come on."

"Who?" asked Stewart. But the two men hurried off, crossing the street at a run.

When they reached Main Street, Gordo halted.

He put an arm against Harve's chest, pushed him back in the shadows of the building next to them.

"There he is," whispered Gordo. "Heading up the street."

"I see him. That the man what laid into us last night?"

"That's him. *Chingon.*"

"Hell, I never got a good look at him. He hit me with a rifle butt or something and knocked my lights plumb out."

"That is the sonofabitch," growled Gordo.

"What're you gonna do, Gordo?"

"Beat the shit out of him, man."

They waited until Gunn was half a block away from them, then Gordo moved out. Harve was right behind him.

Gordo sensed where Gunn was headed. He saw Gunn stop and look in a window, then turned to Harve.

"You get on to the Hog and tell them to come on outside. I'm going to pound me some meat."

"Jake and them?"

Gordo glared at Harve, suddenly angry.

"Hell yes. Jake and Gus. They are drinking or filling their guts with grub. Hurry, man. If you all want to see something. I'm going to take that sonofabitch to the ball."

Harve hurried down the street, never glancing at Gunn, who was on the other side, still peering into a shop window. He passed Gunn, who stood in front of Mossman's General Merchandise, and clambered up the steps of the Hog & Keg. He looked back down the street and didn't see Gordo. But he knew Gordo was there. Waiting for the man he followed to walk on.

Gunn looked at the array of goods in the window. A clerk was shaking a feather duster over a coffee grinder that was painted a bright red. He looked at Gunn and nodded. Gunn smiled. The shop window reminded him of better days, when he and Laurie were in Denver, buying things for their home up on the Poudre. It seemed like a long time ago. And now Laurie was dead, and there was no need for a lone man to have things like coffee grinders, fancy pots and pans, a fireplace grate, whisk brooms and the like. A man's reflection danced by. Gunn didn't turn around.

Gunn turned away from the window. Another reflection almost caused him to pause. But he made no sudden move. Instead, he noted what he had seen and steeled himself to act natural. He recognized the shape of the man across the street. Gordo. And Gordo was standing in shadows, watching him.

And moments before a man had hurried up the street and gone into the Hog & Keg. The first reflection he had seen.

All right. That was probably Harve.

So, those two were up and about. And knew he was there.

It might come to gunplay, and it might not.

But, he would be ready. Harve was probably spilling his guts out inside Larrabee's saloon. And Gordo was lurking across the street like a bull ready to charge.

Gunn crossed the street, headed for the saloon.

Out of the corner of his eye, he saw Gordo closing the distance.

The fat man could move. Gunn saw that his path to the Hog & Keg would be intersected by Gordo before he could reach the board sidewalk. Well, he was damned if he went on, damned if he didn't. He pretended not to see Gordo and continued across the street.

Gordo was moving fast now, almost at a run.

Gunn kept one eye on Gordo, the other on the saloon front. The batwing doors didn't move.

Gunn stopped, then, and whirled on Gordo, his hand flashing to his pistol.

Gordo went into a crouch as he halted.

Gunn's pistol leaped into his hand.

He leveled it at Gordo, hammered back.

Gordo blinked in surprise. His hand was inches away from the butt of his own pistol. He seemed bewildered that Gunn had drawn so fast. Without any apparent effort.

At that moment, the batwing doors swung out and a knot of men clattered boots on the boardwalk.

Jake was in the vanguard and he stopped, staring at Gunn.

"What the hell's goin' on here?" he demanded.

"I just don't like to be drygulched is all," said

Gunn amiably.

"That's the feller I tol' you about, Jake," said Harve. "The one what coldcocked me last night."

"Goddamn you, Harve, I told you to keep your mouth shut about that," snarled Gordo.

"But you said . . ."

"Shut up!" snapped Jake.

Gunn looked over at him and smiled. It was not a warm smile. And his blue-gray eyes turned to a hard pewter. In the shadows, Jake could almost feel the coldness. Like a snake's eyes.

"Remember me?" Gunn asked him.

The muscles on Jake's face shifted. He squinted.

"You the one went for a swim yestiddy?"

"You Jake Early?"

"What of it?"

"They hang horse thieves in Socorro, too?"

"Goddamn you, mister! What're you drivin' at?"

"That dun down at the livery. My horse. Feller said you rode in here."

"Hell, mister, you want sworn testimony? Man sees a horse wanderin' around thouten nobody forkin' him and he adds it to his string. Ain't no crime in that."

Gordo made a slight move.

"I wouldn't do that," Gunn said to Gordo. "This .45 might go off."

Gordo froze, a scowl on his bulging face.

"You got no call to draw down on Gordo," popped up Gus Whitcomb, who moved along the wall so that the three of them wouldn't be in a bunch anymore.

"I don't like sneaks. And that's the second time I

caught this fat Mexican sneaking up on me. You must be Gus Whitcomb."

"Dammit, mister, how come you to know my name? I never set eyes on you before."

Gunn smiled without showing his teeth. It was funny to watch a man lie to you straight out like that. He had them cold. Harve, Jake and Gus. Gordo at bay like a wild boar.

"Bad news has a way of getting around," said Gunn.

The men on the boardwalk started to spread out. The tension hung in the air like smoke, thickened with fear and anticipation.

"One more move," said Gunn, "and I'll drop fatty there first." He held his left palm over the hammer of his Colt, ready to slam the hammer back down if he pulled the trigger. Each man there saw the movement, saw Gunn crouch, ready to fire. Sweat broke out on their foreheads. Gus's hand began to twitch. Jake scowled. Nat Crumb's jaw sagged and his lower lip began to quiver. Only Gordo held fast, unafraid. He leaned forward, as if readying himself for a charge at Gunn.

The tension was broken as a figure appeared behind the batwing doors.

"What's going on out there?"

The three men on the boardwalk turned as one. Gordo's eyes shifted to take in the front of the saloon. Gunn stayed in his killing crouch, saw the man's face out of the corner of his eye.

The batwings swung out and a man stepped through them. He carried a sawed-off double-barreled shotgun in his hands.

"A little trouble, Nate," said Early. "Man threw down on Gordo there. For no damned reason."

"Yeah," said Gus. "He's that Gunn feller."

Larrabee's eyebrows crept up, formed arches. Otherwise he made no sign that he knew who Gunn was.

"Put your pistol away, Mister Gunn," said Larrabee. "This is loaded with double ought buck and the hammers are back."

Gunn's eye swept over, saw the man with the ugly shotgun.

"You tell your men to back off, Larrabee and I'll holster my pistol."

Larrabee considered the proposition.

Seconds ticked by.

"All right, boys, slack off," he said. "Gordo, you go on in, have a drink on me."

Gordo started to say something, bit his lip.

The men on the boardwalk relaxed.

Gunn stood up straight, slipped the Colt back in his holster. Loose.

"Let those hammers down, Larrabee," said Gunn, "and point those barrels down." Gunn's hand hovered near the butt of his Colt.

Larrabee let the hammers down, dipped the barrels toward the dirt.

"Well, Mister Gunn," he said. "We've been expecting you. We've plenty of tar left and I think we can find another bag of feathers."

"You threatening me, Larrabee?"

"Fair warning. You got no business here in Socorro. Best ride on and we'll forget this little incident."

168

A flicker in Larrabee's eyes told Gunn to be careful. The men on the boardwalk hadn't moved and neither had Gordo. Behind him, he heard soft footfalls. To turn would give Larrabee the advantage. And the others could draw and gun him down.

The footsteps came closer.

Then, they were running.

"Get him, Jaime!" yelled Gordo.

Those were the last words Gunn heard as he half-turned. Something cracked down hard on his skull and the sky danced over the tops of the false fronts along Main Street.

From somewhere far off he heard hoarse cries of exultation as his legs turned to jelly and the ground came up to meet him.

CHAPTER THIRTEEN

"Stop it!" shrieked Lorna Starr.

Hurrying to the hotel, she saw Jaime Nieves come out and sneak across the street. In a glance, she saw Larrabee, Jake, Gus, Nat and Gordo all staring at a tall man standing in the street. It took her a moment to realize what was happening. Before she could shout a warning, however, Jaime had raised his rifle, run up to the man and crowned him with the butt. She heard a loud crack and saw the man crumple. The men watching had all cheered.

"Leave that man alone!" she yelled, drawing a small pistol from her handbag.

Jaime paused, the rifle floating above his head, ready to crack down on Gunn's skull a second time.

"Stay out of it, Lorna!" Larrabee said.

"I won't stay out of it! I saw Jaime sneak up on that man and hit him. That was a cowardly deed to say the least. I'll shoot you, Jaime, if you don't leave him alone!"

"*Jefe?* What should I do?" asked Jaime Nieves, a look of bewilderment on his face.

170

Larrabee cursed under his breath.

"Leave the bastard alone. We don't want Lorna mixed up in this."

Jaime lowered his rifle as Lorna came rushing up. Behind her, two men who had seen the entire scene came hurrying along. Lorna stooped and picked up Gunn's head, cradling him in her arms. His hat lay on the ground. There was no blood on Gunn's head, but a lump was slowly swelling. She touched it gingerly, looked up and saw the men coming to her aid.

"Eddy, Bill. Help me get this man over to the Rio Queen. He's hurt."

"Yes'm," said Eddy MacAlwin, who worked as a swamper whenever he was broke. "Bill and I can tote him over there."

Bill Jensen picked up Gunn's hat, swatted it against his leg.

"Mighty cowardly to hit a man from behind like that," he muttered to Lorna.

"You keep quiet, Bill Jensen. We don't want any more trouble here."

Lorna stood up, shook her fist at Larrabee.

"You're the nastiest man I've ever seen," she said. "One of these days you'll get your comeuppance, Nat Larrabee."

"Now, Lorna, let's not indulge in name-calling. That man there threatened my men. Jaime was just putting him down so's he wouldn't get killed accident-like."

"Accident, my foot. You were going to shoot him down."

Indeed, Larrabee had the barrels of the shotgun

up, his thumb on one of the exposed hammers. The other men moved their hands away from their pistols, looked sheepish.

Eddy and Bill lifted Gunn, grunted from the effort.

"A good two hunnert pounds, I'd say," opined Bill.

"Big feller," agreed Eddy. "Where you want us to put him, Miss Lorna?"

Lorna looked at the unconscious man. His eyes were closed, his tousled hair falling over his forehead. His features were slack.

"Take him to my room. Put him in my bed. I'll be there directly. I'm going to the hotel to see how Debbie Barnes is faring."

At that, Jaime spoke in a voice loud enough for Larrabee to hear him. He stood a few paces away from Lorna.

"The woman is *muy enferma.*" he said. "There is much blood. *El Gallo* is there."

Lorna's face blanched. She glared at Larrabee.

"If anything happens to that girl . . ."

Larrabee's mouth curled to a smirk.

"Whatever trouble she's got is her own, Lorna. You better think twice about mixing in."

"I'm not afraid of you, Nat."

Eddy and Bill moved off slowly, carrying the sagging body of Gunn between them.

Lorna wheeled with a flounce of her skirts and started across the street toward the hotel.

Larrabee let the shotgun fall to his side.

"Come on inside, boys. You, too, Jaime. I want to

hear all about the Barnes gal's troubles."

Gordo moved up toward the boardwalk, his fists clenched in anger.

"Let me kill that Gunn now," he begged. "And those who have him."

"Ease on back, Gordo," said Larrabee. "We'll take care of Gunn in due time." He drew a cigar from his vest, stuck it in his mouth. "I think it's time this town learned a good lesson."

He went inside the Hog & Keg, followed by the knot of men. Gordo stopped at the batwings and watched Gunn being carried up the street. His eyes narrowed to porcine slits.

"Come on, Gordo," said Jake. "It's all over."

"We will see, *amigo*," said Gordo. "We will see, eh?"

*   *   *

Gunn's head throbbed.

He was aware of the pain long before he opened his eyes. It started out far away, at some distant point of his consciousness, then drew closer until it was a pounding fist on the walls of his senses. It felt as if he had a crack in his skull and that blood and brains were leaking out. Or was that part of the god-awful dream he'd had moments before? A dream of boulders tumbling off a mountain, burying him in a horrible avalanche, with huge stones slamming into his head, dust suffocating him.

He gasped, opened his eyes.

Stared into the most beautiful face he'd ever seen.

173

Felt the coolness on the egg-sized lump on the back of his head.

"Well, hello there," said a low sweet voice. A voice that caressed his ears like the edges of down feathers. "I was beginning to wonder if you were going to sleep through the day."

Gunn blinked, looked around.

He was in a fine big bed. A soft bed. His shirt was off and his forehead damp.

"Who—who are you . . . ?" he stammered.

"I'm Lorna Starr. And you're Gunn." She pulled her hand away from the back of his head. Gunn saw that there was a damp cloth in it.

"How'd I get here?"

"There'll be time for explanation later. How do you feel? Can you see all right?"

Gunn stared at her. There was no blurring. He may not have a concussion. He remembered very little.

"I can see O.K.," he said. "I feel rotten."

He licked dry lips, looked at the light coming through the shades. Saw the dressing table, the frilly valence on the top of the four-poster. A woman's room, and the scent of perfume was strong in his nostrils. Dried flowers adorned clay vases. There was a roll-top desk, pictures on the walls, some chairs and a small table. A beaded curtain separated the bedroom from the rest of the living quarters.

"You've been out for several hours," said Lorna. "It's late afternoon. I was worried about you."

"Who cracked me on the skull?" Gunn sat up, touched the back of his head gingerly.

174

"Jaime Nieves. He works for Nat Larrabee."

"Who doesn't work for him?"

"I don't. Despite your recent experiences, there are some decent people in Socorro."

"I'm mighty grateful to you for bringing me here."

"I've just come from seeing Debbie Barnes."

Gunn looked into Lorna's deep brown eyes. Her hair was aflame with light; her skin smooth as satin.

"Is she all right?"

"She's weak, but she'll survive, I think. Monica is taking care of her, but as soon as she's stronger, I'm having her move in over here. I have a spare room and she'll be safe. Larrabee has designs on her I'm afraid. I don't quite know why since Caleb is dead, but Jaime was guarding her door when she had the miscarriage."

"Then she lost her baby?"

"Yes. It wasn't very big. No way of telling whether it was boy or girl. I wonder who the father was."

Gunn wasn't about to tell her.

"Maybe you should ask Debbie."

"Maybe I will. Are you hungry?"

"Some."

"I have a proposition for you. I have a parlor. I thought I'd have supper brought up to us. We can have privacy and talk."

"I'd like that . . . Monica . . ."

"Is taking care of Debbie at the hotel. She told me some things about you. Debbie couldn't say much. But I gather you're here because of what Larrabee did to Caleb."

"I am. Do you know anything about it?"

175

Lorna nodded and rose from the bed, went to the window. She raised the shade slightly and pulled the curtains aside.

"Caleb left money in my care. I'll give that to Debbie. Was that what Larrabee was after?"

"No."

"Well, that can wait. Do you want to bathe before supper?"

"Should I?"

Lorna laughed. Her laugh was like her speaking voice: low, throaty, feathery. He liked her. She seemed to be a woman who knew her own mind, who wasn't afraid of the dark and crossing black cats' paths. She lived alone, however, and he supposed that was because most men couldn't hold up under the thought that a woman could do hard things for herself like Lorna apparently had. She owned a saloon, too, which put her against the current. A lot of men would object to a decent woman even being in a saloon, let alone owning one. Lorna went against the grain. She swam upstream when all her peers were swimming down. That was enough to endear her to him. But he was also grateful that she had come along when she had. Otherwise he might be picking feathers out of his hide somewhere down the pike. Like Caleb Barnes.

"I like your smell, Gunn. Funny name for a man. Is it short for . . . what? Gunther? Gunnar? You don't look Scandinavian, though." She turned and looked at him across the room, her eyes scanning his bare chest, the dark hairs that sprouted from the massive expanse of flesh. Gunn felt a tingle run up his spine as if someone had traced a path down it with an icicle.

"Gunnison. I shortened it to make it easier for people to remember. Or forget."

"I rather think I shall remember it."

"You can go ahead and order that supper any time you want, ma'am. I'm fair hungry enough to eat a northbound horse going south."

Lorna laughed. This time her laughter was stronger, lusty like a man's. Her coppery hair shook out, crackling with electricity as she threw her head back.

"You'll have your supper, Gunn. And tell me all about yourself. But don't call me ma'am. It makes me feel old and I'm not yet thirty. I'm Lorna to you and I hope you won't have trouble remembering it."

She left before he could reply, leaving a lingering scent of perfume in the air and the heady musk of woman in his nostrils. She was graceful as a doe in the woods and just as elusive, he thought. From the looks of her, no man had tamed her recently or was likely to soon. She stood taller than most women and she had a bearing that was not common to saloons or cowtowns or dusty trail towns like Socorro.

He wondered about her past. He knew no more about her than when he'd first looked up and seen her face. And she knew more about him than he did about her.

* * *

Larrabee stood at the edge of the ash-strewn property, surveying the remains. He had already sifted through the junk that had been taken to the wash that served as the town dump.

Nothing.

Two men went at the ashes with rakes. The place was picked clean, except for the heavy wood stove that was burned to a crisp. One of the men leaned against it now, toying with the handle of the rake in his hands.

"We been over it ever' foot," said Jake Early, his bootshine marred with ash dust. He still didn't know what the hell Larrabee was looking for—didn't care anymore. This was nigger work.

"No strong box?"

"Nope."

"You look through all the burned books?"

"Looked through 'em. Just burnt pages. Maybe it'd help if I knew what we was lookin' for, Nat?"

"I don't know myself," Larrabee snapped. "Tell Cosgrove there to look inside the stove."

"He did. And I did, about fourteen times."

Larrabee ignored Early's snappish manner. Hell, they were all raw tired. That Gunn being in town didn't help much. Finally he'd gotten the whole story out of Gordo. Gunn had made fools out of his guards. He wondered now if he had come over and found Caleb's journal after he'd knocked Gordo and Harve cold. He could have, but he didn't have any papers on him. A check at the stables had gotten him nowhere. The only place such papers might be if Gunn had taken them would be at Monica Miller's

178

and she wasn't home. Still at the hotel, working or with Debbie Barnes.

Some instinct told him that he'd best slack off as far as she was concerned. Apparently she had been pregnant and miscarried. That was all over town now. He didn't want to stir up people against him. So far he had only run a man out of town. Too bad that Caleb had died, but that wasn't his fault. He was spreading the story now that Caleb had dallied with his own daughter. Smear a dead man's reputation and he couldn't argue nor deny it. Part of the story he was circulating was that Caleb had owed him money, refused to pay it and threatened him—so he had been tarred and feathered. People respected a man who paid his debts and he meant to see that Caleb Barnes looked like a dishonest and immoral man. That way, when he ran Lorna Starr out, he'd have the town locked up. There was a lot of money to be made in Socorro, but not enough to go around. Not the kind of money he needed. Lorna was cutting into his business bad. On the last trail drive, most of the drovers had flattened their asses on her bar stools, played their poker hands on her tables, left their pokes in her till. The bitch!

"All right, Jake," said Larrabee, "tell Cosgrove to pack it in. You boys come on and have a drink."

"What d'you figger to do about that Gunn jasper?" Early asked.

"Oh, I'm not worried about it," he said lightly. But his brows knitted up and his eyes narrowed. "He'll wear out his welcome soon enough."

"He's goin' to come after me over those saddlebags and that horse."

"You worried, Jake?"

"Some. That *hombre* ain't rightly human. I dusted his pate down at the river and he should have drowned like a rat. Instead, he comes out of the ground like a ghost and beats the shit out of Gordo, puts a knot in Harve's head and then braces me where I damned sure live."

"Just bluff."

"Yeah? Well, the boys don't think so. Nate Crumb sayd he heard of someone with that name up in Wyoming territory. Worked for the Cattle Association there. Put a lot of hard men six feet under."

"I heard that. Just talk. Trail gossip. Let me worry about Gunn. Mind your back, but don't go lookin' for trouble. He'll come out of his hole soon enough."

Larrabee didn't want his men getting nervous about Gunn. He'd heard the talk too, and some of it made sense. He'd heard a tale or two himself. Not only about Wyoming, but about Colorado and Taos. Back in San Francisco he'd heard a story from a Chinese gal named Soo Li that had curled his hair. He wondered now if that was the same Gunn. If so, he was hell on wheels. Men like that didn't come along very often.

His big worry was not who Gunn was or where he'd been, but what Caleb had told him. Was Gunn here to look for that journal? Or had Caleb told him the whole story? Had he had time, before he died, to tell Gunn what he had found out, stumbled upon? It was likely. But if so, Gunn would have gotten help, gone to the telegraph up in Santa Fe. Wouldn't he?

Or braced him instead of Jake Early? It was puzzling right now. Best to keep his mouth shut and see what move Gunn made next.

Early walked away, spoke to Cosgrove. Cosgrove carried the rakes, saluted as he walked back to the Hog & Keg. Jake came over to walk back with Larrabee.

"Gordo wants a piece of Gunn's hide," Jake said. "Maybe we ought to sic him on Gunn."

"No," Larrabee said. "Let's see what Gunn's next move is. He's probably got a headache and won't bother us much for a day or so."

"You're the boss," said Early, matching Larrabee's stride as the two men walked down the street. The sun was hanging over the horizon, throwing long shadows across the dirt. The temperature was dropping slowly and there was a light breeze picking up. The adobes all looked pink and gold depending on the shade and the sky was a pale blue.

Larrabee didn't want Gunn shot down just yet. First he had to find out what the man knew. What Caleb might have told him. If Gunn had a hand, he'd show it. If he didn't, he'd poke around, ask questions and then there would be time enough to take him down.

Larrabee looked back at the empty spot on the street once. A tuft of wind stirred up the ashes. Maybe the journal had burned up in the fire. Maybe there was no tin box or safe. Maybe Caleb had been bragging. Whistling in the dark. To save his skin.

No, Caleb had known. The man hadn't been a liar. He had found out about him, and he'd written it down. But God only knew where that journal was. And whoever had it would die. No questions asked.

Larrabee hoped it would be Gunn.

* * *

Monica went into the room, lit a lamp by Debbie's bed side.

Julieta was asleep in a chair.

Something moved and Monica shot a hand to her mouth, startled. She looked past the light thrown by the lamp and saw him there, standing in the shadows. A cold chill clutched at her stomach, electrified her spine.

"El Gallo!" she whispered. "What are you doing here?"

The medicine man stepped out of the shadows, his face impassive.

She repeated her question in Spanish.

He shook a fist at her. The fist clutched a quill rattle, a hollow turkey feather filled with gravel. The sound it made was like a rattlesnake. Monica stepped back, suddenly frightened.

"Evil spirits are here. Around that girl who has had much bleeding. You are in danger. Much danger."

"Go on home, old man!"

"I will go, but you must beware. There is bad medicine here."

"*Vaya!*"

The old man shuffled past her, floated out the door. The air seemed musty in the room. The candle flickered, almost went out. The flame threw skulking shadows across the walls. Monica shut the door, looked at Debbie's pale face. She looked exhausted, almost dead, with the sallow light touching one side of her face. The dresser had been moved away, the room picked up, but the smell of medicines mingled with the musty scent of *El Gallo's* presence.

Julieta had not awakened.

"I'll be back later," Monica whispered, as if to reassure the two women who could not hear her.

The silence creaked in the room.

Monica opened the door, stepped into the dark hall. No lamps had been lit yet. A floorboard creaked.

She turned, saw a man's head loom up out of the shadows.

A hood hid the man's features.

"What . . . ?"

A hand floated out to her face, clamped over her mouth.

She felt herself being pushed backwards. Another pair of hands grabbed at her. Arms went around her waist.

Monica struggled. Tried to scream.

Then, she felt herself being dragged along the hall. Not toward the stairs, but to another room. She tried to bite the hand over her mouth.

Something hard slammed into her head.

Shooting stars exploded behind her eyes. She heard a door slam.

Someone shoved her and she fell onto the bed. She turned over, stared, saw the hooded men surrounding her. She gasped with fear.

One of the men came toward her, an air of familiarity about him.

"One scream," he said, "and I'll cut your gizzard out."

And Monica began to pray silently.

CHAPTER FOURTEEN

Lorna Starr leaned over the table toward Gunn. Her low-cut bodice revealed the soft spheres of her breasts straining at the taffeta cloth of her emerald-green gown. A single candle glowed at the center of the table, flickering warmly, lighting her nut-brown eyes.

"More potatoes?"

Gunn shook his head, surveyed the lavish spread. He'd put away two thin beefsteaks, a mountain of potatoes, several biscuits spread with butter and honey, several helpings of creamed nickel-sized carrots, and half a bottle of red wine.

"You said you had a proposition for me," he said, pushing away from the table. The *mozo* appeared with more steaming coffee, filled their cups. He looked at Lorna who waved him away. The parlor was cozy, intimate. The table had been set up in the middle of the room, which was circular, had two bead-curtain entrances. They were on the second floor of the Rio Queen. Distant sounds of laughter and tinkling glasses drifted to their ears, but it seemed to Gunn as if they were in a different world.

The walls had been covered with red felt, the furniture wood gleamed with polishing oils, and there was crystal everywhere he looked.

Lorna reached for a decanter of brandy, poured two glasses. She handed one to Gunn.

"I do. Especially now that I know more about you. But, first, a toast."

"Yes?" Gunn lifted the brandy snifter.

"To the new town marshal," she said, a smile flickering on her full lips.

"No," said Gunn.

Lorna frowned.

"No?"

"I don't hire out my gun."

"Not even for legal purposes?"

"Sometimes. But this is a lawless town, from all I've seen. I came here to find something, to carry out a promise. I don't want gunplay. I don't want to be a target."

"You are a target, Gunn."

"Maybe. But I've never hid behind a badge yet and I don't want to now."

"You sound bitter."

"Not bitter. Realistic. I've known a few lawmen. Most of them good men. Honest, even. At first. Until town politics catches up with them. And, there's another side to the law."

"Which is . . ."

"Most bad men and lawmen are cut from the same cloth. They pick different sides, but play the same game. It's like kids playing sheriff and outlaw. Only difference is the badge. Underneath, they're all criminals."

"I know what you mean. I've just never heard it expressed out loud."

"I'll propose a toast," said Gunn. "To you, pretty lady. For a fine meal and uncommon company."

They clinked their snifters and drank of the brandy. Lorna held her glass with delicate long fingers, the nails immaculately polished. The veins and muscles in her neck stood out as she drank. She was a rare beauty and Gunn meant his toast to compliment her. The brandy warmed him and he longed to reach out, touch her hand, draw her close to him and discover the fire behind those lips of hers. But he was too much of a gentleman to take advantage of her hospitality.

It was early, but the sun had gone down.

"Would you like to smoke?" she asked, as the *mozo* returned to clear off the dishes. "I have some cigars in a humidor."

"No. Maybe later. I'm sorry to have to turn you down, Lorna. I don't intend to stay long here and you know how I feel about a badge."

"Yes," she said sadly. "I didn't really expect you to settle here. And, it was presumptuous of me to hope that you would accept the job of town marshal. The last one we had did not fare so well."

"Lorenzo Miller?"

"Yes."

"What happened to him?"

"Didn't Monica tell you? He was killed. Under mysterious circumstances."

"She said he was murdered."

"Probably."

"Any idea who did it?"

Lorna shook her head.

"Let's move to the settee," she said, rising from the table. "Bring your glass with you."

They sat on a love seat. Lorna was close. The *mozo* moved the brandy decanter over to a side table.

The tinkly music of a piano drifted up the stairs. Somewhere, a dog barked.

The *mozo* finished up his work, lit a lamp, blew out the candle after he removed the linen tablecloth.

Gunn heard a door slam. The piano music grew muffled. The laughter faded away.

Lorna poured more brandy.

"If you won't take a marshal's badge, will you at least work for me?" Lorna asked, after a while. "I'll make it worth your while."

Gunn considered it. He needed freedom, but he also needed to blend into the scenery for a while.

"What did you have in mind?"

"I need a dealer. Are you good with cards?"

"Fair. I'm no gambler, though."

Lorna laughed that low laugh of hers.

"I can teach you what you need to know. We run an honest house here, but there are some finer points you should know."

"I know how to catch seconds, thirds, fourths."

"Yes, I'm sure you do," she mused. "Well?"

Gunn looked at her, saw the look in her eyes. She put an arm up on the back of the settee. Her fingers touched his shoulder. Just barely. Her breasts moved up and down in the green taffeta dress. With any luck, they might pop out. Only the nipples held them back. Gunn felt a swarm of heat in his loins. He looked away quickly, set his glass down on the other side table.

"I'm afraid I'll have to turn you down there, too. I have something else in mind, Lorna."

"I said I'd make it worth your while, Gunn."

The pause was pregnant with meaning.

"I know."

"Will you consider it? I'd like to have you on my side."

"I am on your side, I think."

"In my camp, then."

She set her snifter down, scooted closer to Gunn. The scent of her perfume was strong in his nostrils. She offered him her lips. Her eyes closed.

Gunn took her in his arms, kissed her.

His senses swam as her tongue entered his mouth. Intimately. Searching, probing. Like a finger. The heat in his loins turned to raw fire. His manhood throbbed with a sudden rush of engorging blood. His trousers stretched at the crotch, bulged.

He ran his own tongue into her mouth. Tongue-to-tongue, they kissed. It was a long kiss. An exploring one.

Gunn lifted a hand, found the edge of her gown. He ran a finger underneath, down the edge to the soft mound of her breast. He gave a gentle tug. Felt the garment loosen. The breast flowed free and his fingertip touched the rubbery nipple. It was hard as a thumb.

He did the same with the other side. Cupped the other breast in his warm palm.

Lorna sighed, bit him softly on his lower lip. There was no pain, just a shot of ice through his system. The ice hit the fire, churned his blood. His cock pulsed with fresh blood.

"Why did you do that?" she husked, a moment later.

"Curiosity."

She laughed again. The laugh so low it tugged at him. He touched her face with his fingers. Her skin was as delicate as parchment. He touched her full lips, traced his finger back and forth.

Lorna looked down at her exposed breasts.

"They look better that way," said Gunn.

"Yes. They do. No one has ever touched me that way. No one has ever been this bold with me."

"Maybe someone should have."

"Maybe. Are you trying to seduce me, Gunn?"

"Do you want to be seduced?"

"Yes. I think so."

She put an arm around his neck, drew his head to hers. Kissed him hard on the mouth.

Again, the surge of blood. Blood singing in his temples, ringing dim bells. He wanted her. Wanted her bad.

He rubbed her breasts. Felt her respond.

"I think it would be easier if I got out of this dress. If we went into the bedroom."

"Yes," he said, his voice scratchy with desire.

She led him into the bedroom, lighted a lamp. The beads still rattled from their passing.

"Will anyone . . . ?"

"No one will come up here," she said. "The door to the parlor is closed. I can lock it if you're nervous."

"If you're not, I'm not."

She laughed again.

"Does this mean you're accepting my offer?" she challenged.

"No. It means I want you, that's all."

"Undress me, Gunn. I don't think I have the strength. Or the courage."

He laughed, looked at her plump breasts jutting free of the gown. Perfectly formed. Beautiful. The nipples protruding, excited to an acorn hardness. He slipped her gown from her shoulders, watched it flow to the floor. She stepped out of the puddle of green taffeta, stood there in panties and stockings. Black silk stockings held up by shiny green and black garters of silk. Black ribbons and bows, green silk with elastic inside.

She kicked off her shoes and sat on the bed.

Gunn slithered out of his buckskins, wrestled with his boots. When he was naked, he saw that she still sat there, in stockings and panties, more naked than if she had removed them.

She stretched out one leg tauntingly.

Gunn knelt down, pulled at the garter. He rolled the stocking down, slipped it off her foot.

Lorna extended her other leg.

Gunn removed garter and stocking.

Lorna leaned back, bracing herself on her elbows. Thrust her thighs at him. Her panties were pink, silken. He saw the dark patch underneath. Fine tendrils of hairs growing out at the elasticized sides. He pulled gently on the top, slipped the panties down below her belly button. Then slid them down to her legs, gazing at the pubic patch.

She was a real redhead.

He dropped the panties on top of the black

silk stockings.

Lorna slid further onto the bed. He climbed in beside her, began to fondle her breasts. She grabbed his cock, squeezed it. He kissed a breast, took the nipple into his mouth. Worried it with his tongue.

Lorna squirmed on the bed. She had long fine legs. Her skin had a beautiful texture to it. It was very smooth. As fine a skin as he'd ever seen. Smooth and flawless, like snows high in the mountains.

"This is very sudden, you know," she said.

"Yes. Good things are sudden sometimes."

"And bad, as well."

"Yes. Want to change your mind?"

"No," she said quickly. "I couldn't stop now. Even if I wanted to."

"You could."

"No!" And tears came to her eyes. As quickly as they came, they stopped, as if she was fighting with herself. As if she had held her emotions in for so long that she couldn't release them without an inner struggle.

Gunn slid next to her, kissed her mouth. Their tongues tangled again. Lorna squirmed. Her hand squeezed his manhood harder than before.

He kissed her all over, as she writhed with pleasure. He kissed her between her legs and she squealed. He let his tongue probe her. He tasted of her heat, smelled her heady musk.

She bucked with orgasm and his tongue slid deeper into the steaming folds of pink flesh. The wiry brass hairs scratched his face. Her leg pressed against his head, smothered him.

Her legs went wide and he crawled atop her.

"Now?" he asked.

"Now! Oh, Gunn, what are you doing to me?"

"Loving you," he said quietly as he slid inside, piercing her with his swollen shaft.

* * *

The knock on the door was loud, insistent.

It jarred them out of their lassitude.

"I'll see who it is," said Lorna, her voice sleepy.

Gunn watched her as she glided to a wardrobe, pulled out a silken robe. She whispered across the room, through the beaded doorway. He heard the door squeak open. Voices. One of them was a man's. High-pitched. Familiar. Excited. He slid off the bed, suspecting trouble. It was too bad. He wanted Lorna again. The bed was roiled with blankets and sheets, rank with the scents of their lovemaking.

He was pulling on his boots when Lorna came back, her face chalk.

"Who was it?" he asked.

"Pepito Salazar. He works at the hotel. He's worried. Monica didn't go home at her usual time. Julieta hasn't seen her. There are no lamps lit in her house."

"Why did he come here?"

"He knew you were here. He thought she might have come with you."

Gunn's eyebrows went up.

"Small town," he said.

"Yes," she smiled. "Gunn, I'm worried. Larrabee may have . . ."

193

"I know. I'll go with Pepito. Check it out."

"Thanks." She put a hand on his arm.

"I hate to leave so sudden."

"Just come back," she whispered, touching his lips with her index finger.

He grabbed her, kissed her in farewell.

Then, he was gone.

*　*　*

Pepito was in a state of extreme agitation when Gunn let himself out of Lorna's parlor. He wrung his hands, babbled on in Spanish and English about the *señora*.

"Keep it, Pepito. We'll backtrack and see what we can find. Did you go inside her house? Maybe she was asleep. She must be pretty tired about now."

"Yes. She might be asleep. I did not go in. But I am the one who always walks her home. She did not come to get me. I am very worried, *Señor*. If anything has happened to the *señora* . . ."

"Don't blame yourself. Let's wait. Maybe nothing's happened to her."

But Gunn had a sinking feeling in his gut. Monica seemed to be a creature of habit. If she had Pepito escort her to and from the hotel she would not vary from that routine without an explanation. If she had wanted to go home alone she would have at least told him so. No, something was damned wrong!

Pepito led the way down the back stairs. Gunn caught a glimpse of men at the bar and tables, saw a woman or two in the crowd. The piano was making music and there was the flutter of shuffled cards, the clank of glasses, the ring of money on the wooden bar.

Outside, it was not as cold as the night before. The stairs went down the side of the building, deposited them near the boardwalk on Main Street.

"Where do we go first?" Pepito asked.

"To Monica's. The quickest, shortest way. She might be there."

Monica's house was dark. There was no one across the street, Gunn noted. The street was quiet. He knocked loudly on the front door. Pepito was trembling, babbling again. Perhaps, Gunn thought, he was saying more prayers for Monica's safety.

He tried the door.

Locked.

They went around to the back, where Gunn knocked again. No answer. He looked at the door, saw that there were marks on it. He worked the latch. The door swung open.

Gunn went in. Pepito hesitated.

"Come on. See if you can find a lamp and light it."

Pepito came in, hurried to the kitchen. A moment later, Gunn heard a match being struck. The clatter of a glass chimney. The lamp wick caught and the room danced with shadows. Pepito put the chimney back. It rattled in the Mexican's shaking hand.

"Hold it high," Gunn said, looking around.

The kitchen was a mess. Cupboards gaping open, flour spilled onto the counter. Coffee on the floor. The stove doors open wide.

"Come on," Gunn said grimly, "let's take a look at the rest of the house."

They had ransacked it. Every room. Sheets were

ripped off the bed, the wardrobe in a shambles. They had even searched through the fireplace. The morning's ashes were all over the hearth, the floor. They hadn't been too careful about it, either.

Gunn's anger boiled over.

"Those bastards," he cursed.

There was no sign of Monica.

Nor any sign that she had even been there. Gunn went over every inch of the place carefully.

Outside, he sucked in a breath.

"What do we do now?" Pepito asked.

Gunn looked at his shadowy face in the darkness, tried to think.

"You say she never came to get you in the hotel?"

"*Si.* I mean no. I have not seen her in many hours."

"When was the *last* time you saw her?"

"She was working at the desk. Then, she went upstairs to see about the girl. I did not see her come down."

A light flashed in Gunn's brain.

"Damn!" he said. "Come on, Pepito!"

They trotted to the hotel. Gunn had a stitch in his side when he finally went inside, Pepito dogging his heels.

"Take me to Debbie Barnes' room," he said.

A wizened desk clerk looked at them both, saw Pepito and bent his head back down to his books. Gunn climbed the stairs three steps at a time behind the scrambling Salazar.

"This is the girl's room," Pepito said, stopping before a closed door.

Gunn drew his pistol, knocked on the door.

196

"Un momento," came a woman's voice from the other side.

The door opened a crack, then closed quickly.

"Open it!" Gunn said.

"Who is it?"

"Gunn!"

The door opened wide.

Gunn saw a startled woman. He put away his gun as he saw Debbie lift an arm. He swept past the woman, went to Debbie.

"What is it?" she asked weakly.

"I'm looking for Monica. She's disappeared."

"Monica? Why?"

Julieta intruded between Gunn and the bed.

"You leave us alone. This woman is very sick. She could start bleeding again if you . . ."

"Who are you?" Gunn asked.

Julieta told him. He realized that she was right. Debbie was pale as a lily.

"Have you seen Monica?"

"No. But I was awakened a few hours ago. I heard noises. Here in the room. When I fell asleep *El Gallo* was here. I thought maybe he had made noise when he was leaving."

"Or maybe someone came in here and got Monica," said Gunn, whirling. "Talk to you later, Debbie. Get some rest."

Pepito closed the door behind him.

Gunn stood there, thinking.

"Where do you look now?" Pepito asked.

"All right. She didn't go home. She didn't go back down to her desk. So, she must be up here some-where. We'll start knocking on doors. You take one side, I'll take the other."

Halfway down the hall, Gunn heard something. A muffled cry.

He tried the door. Locked. He broke it down, crunching into it with a lowered shoulder, driving with his legs. With his anger.

"Jesus!" he exclaimed as he burst inside the room.

Monica lay on the bed, a gag in her mouth. Her legs and arms spreadeagled.

He almost didn't recognize her.

CHAPTER FIFTEEN

Monica moaned.

Gunn dashed to her, took the gag out of her mouth.

She sucked in lifegiving air.

A lamp flickered on the dresser. The room reeked of whiskey, stale tobacco. There was a bottle on the table, an ashtray full of cigarette and cigar butts.

Pepito entered the room cautiously. He gasped when he saw his mistress.

"Dios mio," he breathed.

"Shut the door, Pepito," said Gunn. "And keep your eyes peeled. Whoever was in here might come back."

Monica shook her head. Cried out with the pain of movement.

Gunn started to untie her hands first. He could hardly bear to look at her. Her face was swollen, bruised. One cheek was a swollen purple lump. She was naked to her waist.

The bastards had put hot cigarettes to her breasts. Tortured her.

The bile of hatred and disgust rose up in Gunn's

throat. He untied the other knot on her wrist, then went to the foot of the bed to free her feet. There were cigarette burns on her legs, as well.

"Thank God you're here, Gunn," said Monica. The words were distorted, spoken with bruised puffy lips. Lips cracked where someone's fist had cracked against the delicate flesh. Gunn winced to see her pain.

"I'm here. You're safe now. Can you talk without too much pain? What happened?"

He helped her sit up, had Pepito fetch her a glass of water. There was a pitcher and glass on the dresser. She drank it greedily. She put her dress back on her shoulders, shook with the pain of using her arms. These, too, were bruised.

Sobbing, she told him what had happened.

"Did you get a look at any of them?"

She shook her head.

"Did you recognize any of the voices?"

"I—I can't be sure. They—they disguised them, I'm sure."

"What did they want?"

"I don't know. A box. Some papers."

"A journal?"

"Yes. I think so. They wanted to know if you brought anything to the house when you were there. I told them no, but they didn't believe me. Gunn, they kept hitting me and burning me. I—I couldn't scream . . ."

He sat on the bed with her, put his arms gently around her shoulders.

"Don't think about it now," he said softly. "We're going to get you home. Pepito will stay there with you."

"Can't you stay?"

"No. I don't think that's wise. It might be best if you forgot about me for a while. They've been to your house. Ransacked it."

"Oh!"

"Pepito can straighten it up. Maybe you'd like to have a woman with you . . ."

"No. I—I can manage. They didn't break anything. They—they just hurt me. Shamed me."

But she didn't cry again. Gunn marveled at her inner strength. He helped get her out of bed. She could walk, but he and Pepito helped her until she steadied. He was shocked at her appearance. The dimples that had made her so comely were all smudged. Whoever had worked her over had done it with finesse. And cruelty. And he was to blame. He had no use for men who hid behind masks or bandannas. And less use for men who beat up on women. His first instinct was to tear the town apart, but he knew that wasn't the way to accomplish anything. The best thing to do now was to keep a cool head. Maybe Larrabee was responsible. It looked that way. But he was smart. Smart enough to keep his identity hidden. Something about the man had scratched a memory. His talk, the way he stood. The short-barreled shotgun. There was a familiarity about him that Gunn couldn't define. Not yet. It wasn't his face. He had never laid eyes on the man before. But another thing. Something he had heard somewhere. A fragment. A scrap of something.

They walked down the hall. Gunn stopped in at Debbie's room.

He held her hand, talked quietly to her.

"Monica was hurt. She'll be all right. I'll see you in the morning."

Julieta hovered over her patient, eyeing Gunn suspiciously.

"What happened?" Debbie asked.

"Someone's still looking for your pa's journal."

"Have you . . . ?"

"Not yet. I'll take it slow. You get some rest, Debbie."

"Gunn," she said. "Thank you. Thank you for coming by. I . . ."

Gunn looked at Julieta, the midwife.

"I'll be goin'. You rest easy. Goodnight, *Señora.*"

Julieta's look softened. Gunn gave Debbie's hand a squeeze, left the room. He helped Monica and Pepito get down the stairs.

"What are you going to do, Gunn?" she asked, when they were in the lobby.

"Get to know Larrabee."

"I don't understand."

"It won't look good, Monica, but trust me. It's the only way. Right now I'm a target. The only way to clear things up, take off the pressure, is to beard the lion in his den."

"You're going to kill Larrabee?"

"No. Not yet, anyway."

"Then, what?"

"I'm going to ask him for a job."

* * *

The Hog & Keg was noisy, smoke-filled, bright

202

and dangerous.

When Gunn walked through the batwing doors, a dozen pair of eyes swept his way, locked on him. There was a momentary hush as he strode through the doors, headed for the long bar on the left. The piano player turned around, stopped his hands in mid-air. The fiddle player hit a sour note. The banjo man's fingers slipped off the frets.

A tiny moment of silence.

Jake Early stepped away from the bar, reeling slightly.

Nate Crumb coughed nervously.

Gus Whitcomb scraped his chair as he slid away from the poker table, his hand floating above his pistol.

Gunn ignored the attention.

He slid his hat back on his head, swung a leg up on the brass rail.

The bartender hesitated until he met Gunn's cold pewter gaze.

Gunn fished out a cartwheel, tapped it on the bar.

"Whiskey," he said. "Two fingers."

The sounds came back into mesh. The piano tinkled again, the fiddler sawed his instrument. The banjo player plunked in rhythm. Cards whisk-whicked and chips clacked. Glasses were raised and eyes shifted away from the tall man at the end of the bar. A few sidelong glances struck him as he surveyed the room. Early stared at him, wondering.

"The boss man in?" Gunn asked the barkeep when he brought the whiskey.

"Mister Larrabee? He's in."

"Like to talk to him."

"Mister, I'll ask if he wants to talk to you."

"Fair enough," said Gunn, ignoring the barkeep's surly manner. The balding man went down to the end of the bar, whispered something to Jake Early. Jake shot Gunn a hard glance, then left the bar. He went to a back room, knocked, then disappeared inside. He hadn't staggered, Gunn noticed. Apparently the man had the ability to control himself somewhat when drinking. It was a point worth noting. A lot of men could draw on some reserve when pressed, even when drinking too much liquor.

Gus Whitcomb went back to his game, but he kept one eye on Gunn.

Nathan Crumb walked over to another table, sat down facing Gunn. He kept one of his hands under the table.

Gunn saw a man go up on the small stage, hold his arms up.

"Gents, Miss Abby Harris will sing for your pleasure in just five minutes. Order your drinks now. No orders when the lady's singing."

There was a smattering of applause.

A moment later, Jake Early came back out, started walking toward Gunn.

Gunn finished his drink.

"Larrabee says come on back. I'll take your pistol."

"I'll keep it, Early."

"Suit yourself. I'll be right behind you. You even twitch, I'll hole your back."

Gunn didn't argue with the man. He kept his eyes on Whitcomb and Crumb, walked back to the office. The door was open.

Nat Larrabee sat behind a desk. The office was sparse, functional. There was a large safe, a liquor bar, couch, low table, some chairs. A pretty woman with too much rouge on her cheeks and thick eyelashes sat on the couch, her legs crossed. She wore mesh stockings, the garters showing under the short skirt. The thighs provocatively visible. Her hair was done up in thick curls, laced with a blue ribbon. Her skimpy dress was shiny satin, her lips cherry red, her eyes blue.

"Gunn. You wanted to see me?"

Gunn looked at Early, frowned.

"Leave us be, Jake," said Larrabee. "Close the door, but stick around outside. In case I need you."

Jake frowned, nodded. He didn't like being kicked out, but there was nothing he could do about it.

Gunn still didn't say anything. He looked at the woman on the couch, who was smoking a pre-rolled cigarette in a long holder. She blew a spool of smoke out toward Gunn, looked at him, her eyebrows arched questioningly.

"This is Miss Abby Harris," said Larrabee. "She's just going on, aren't you, Abby?"

Abby snubbed out her cigarette in a pewter ashtray and minced out of the room, going through a door that led backstage.

"Have a chair, Gunn."

Larrabee seemed wary, but not ill-at-ease. He was, rather, curious. He picked up an empty rifle shell from his desk, began toying with it.

Gunn pulled up a chair, leaned back, stretching his legs.

"I came here to ask you for a job, Larrabee."

Larrabee's face showed no change of expression. "Oh?"

"I'm broke. And if I don't get my horse back from Early, afoot to boot."

"Yes. I suppose that's true. I'm sure you need a job. But I'm not sure about your loyalties. Seems to me you mixed in something that didn't concern you and now you're crawling."

"Not crawling. I just like to be on the winning side. Miss Starr offered me a job. I turned her down."

Now Larrabee's expression softened. He leaned over the desk, twiddling with the brass shell casing.

"She want to hire you for your gun?"

"And other things."

Larrabee laughed, a roaring guffaw that made his face redden. He reared back and slapped his knee. The empty shell clattered on the desk top.

"Be damned! Lorna's a case ace. Tricky as a Mexican surveyor."

"Yep, I figger I'm in enough trouble over one woman, I'd best stay clear of that one. Oh, I'm grateful to her for keeping me from getting my head bashed in by your boys, but that's as far as it goes. What about it, Larrabee? Can you use a good man who can take orders, keep his mouth shut?"

Larrabee stopped laughing, composed himself.

"I don't know, Gunn. My boys won't take it none too good if I hire you on. They got some grudge against you."

"I'll make my peace with them."

Larrabee swung around in his chair, looked at a crack in the wall. He seemed to be considering the matter.

"Can you deal a hand of cards?"

"I can deal 'em fair or dirty."

Larrabee smiled.

Stood up and stretched out a hand.

"You go on the payroll. Got a place to stay?"

Gunn shook his hand and his head.

"Some of the boys bunk at the hotel or at a place I got up the street. Take your pick. Feel like starting tonight?"

"Sooner the better. Early got my poke too."

"Well, now, you and Jake can work things out I'm sure. You relieve Baldy at table number three. You can't miss him. Give him this card." Larrabee opened a desk drawer, drew out a pink shift card. It had some signatures on it. Gunn took it, tipped his hat.

"Mighty obliged," he said.

He heard Larrabee chuckling when he left. Jake went in the office and Gunn walked out on the floor, started looking for Baldy's table. He held the pink card up so Gus and Nate Crumb could see it plain.

Baldy seemed surprised when Gunn came up, handed him the card.

"You workin' here, Bud?"

"The name's Gunn. I am. Take your break."

"Well, all right, Gunn. Watch the fellow with the blue bandanna. He plays a tight hand."

Gunn sat in, started dealing. A few minutes later, the game stopped as the four-piece band struck up an overture. Someone lit the stage candles. The curtains opened and Abby Harris stepped out front. The band went into a vamp and she began to sing.

She looked at Gunn through the whole song, a cloying ballad of lost love and death in a mining camp. There were only a few dry eyes in the place. She danced, sang and joked with the men and women, finally coming down into the audience where she flirted with several men. Finally, she sat on Gunn's lap, ran her fingers through his hair.

Larrabee and Jake Early watched from the bar. Larrabee was smiling. Early was not.

When her numbers were over, the games started up again. Gunn worked until midnight, when he was relieved by Baldy. He had done well, cleaning out the man with the blue bandanna. Baldy patted him on the back.

"Boss wants to see you," he said.

Gunn found Larrabee at the bar.

"Buy you a drink, Gunn?"

"I'd take it."

"You deal a fine hand. Glad you joined us. You like Abby?"

"She sings right nice."

"She'd like you to see her home. And, I've got your saddlebags in my office. Jake's not a dumb man. He listens to reason now and then."

Gunn smiled, drank his whiskey.

Things were working out well. At least on the surface. He wasn't fooling himself however. Larrabee was no fool. He hadn't hired Gunn out of the goodness of his heart. Rather, he had done so to keep an eye on him. Which was all right with Gunn. He was just where he wanted to be.

* * *

208

Abby Harris fluffed her blonde curls, put a key in the door to the house.

"Come on up," she said. "This is where you'll stay."

"I don't get it," he said.

"This is the house that Nat owns. Some of the boys stay here. I live alone on the top floor."

"Where's my room?"

"Downstairs. But you won't be needing it tonight."

Dumbfounded, Gunn went inside with her. It was dark, but Abby didn't light a lamp. He followed her blindly up the stairs. The house was a huge, three-storied adobe, with a balcony. It looked almost like a mission without the bell tower. He couldn't see the furnishings, but it smelled nice inside. Abby was right. The whole top floor was hers. She locked the door to the stairs and lit a lamp in the parlor. She carried it into the large living room.

The decor was Spanish. Mexican. Home-made furniture, lots of blankets, pottery. A fireplace, mantel. Indian rugs woven on ancient looms. Hopi, or Navajo, he guessed.

"Have a drink with me?"

"Yes. Do you always bring the new man up to your rooms?"

Abby's eyes flashed. She whirled and slapped him hard on the face. Gunn didn't flinch.

"How dare you! I asked you here because I thought you were a gentleman!"

"I am. Sometimes. You move pretty fast though."

She looked as if she was going to strike him again. Gunn smiled warmly at her. She smiled back.

"Let's not have a drink," she purred. "Let's go

straight to bed. I'm tired of being pawed over by drunks and stared at by loonies. Kiss me."

He kissed her and she turned into a tigress.

It was all he could do to get her to the bedroom. She undressed quickly and left her clothes strewn all over the room. She blew out the lamp and they lay together in darkness. She crawled all over him, mewling and purring, like a cat.

When he entered her, she was even more savage.

She bit and clawed, thrashed wildly.

She seemed to have one continuous orgasm from the moment he first touched her. He had heard about such women before, but had never met one. He didn't know the word for it. But when he climaxed, she wouldn't leave him alone. She wanted him again.

He mounted her and she rolled over so that she was on top.

She slid up and down on his oiled shaft faster than any woman he'd ever seen. She cried and screamed, scratched at his face as if to leave her mark on him. He fought for control and finally rolled her back where he wanted her. Then, he took her with a savagery of his own until she screamed so loud he was sure she would wake the town.

When it was over, he rolled away, his body soaked with sweat.

"Jesus, but you're good," she breathed. "Finally. A real man."

"You don't have a man?"

"No. Have you seen them? There was only one real man here and he's dead."

Gunn was afraid to ask.

But he did.

"Who would that be?"

"Oh, someone I knew once. He was married. He satisfied me, though. Poor Lonny. I wish he were still alive."

"Yeah. I didn't know him." Gunn's mouth was dry. He had a cold steel ball in his stomach.

"You would have liked him." She paused. "But, you're better. Much better. I'm glad you're here. Stay with me, please. Don't sleep downstairs."

"Maybe you'd sleep better if I did."

She laughed. A throaty laugh that was like a tigress purring.

A few minutes later, she was at him again.

Gunn didn't know if he had anything left.

He didn't know who Abby Harris was, but she was insatiable. One of those women no man could satisfy. Not ten men. Not a dozen. Nor a hundred.

But one man had, once.

Lonny.

Lorenzo Miller.

Monica's dead husband!

CHAPTER SIXTEEN

Gunn worked a full week for Larrabee before he got a day off.

Work was a relief to him. The nights were sodden lusty orgies with Abby that left him red-eyed in the mornings. She did sleep, he found out. Almost all day. It took him a couple of days to adjust to her nightowl schedule. He never did find out which room was supposed to be his. He knew only that Jake and Gus stayed there and Nate Crumb lived at the hotel.

The toughest part was facing Lorna Starr.

He met her on the street the afternoon of his day off. He tried to avoid her, but she came up to him boldly, an accusation in her eyes.

"Well, I see now why you didn't want to work for me," she said bitterly.

"It wouldn't have worked out," he said laconically.

People passing by stared at them.

"Will you at least have some coffee with me?"

"I think not," he said, knowing that some of the

eyes on him belonged to men who worked for Larrabee.

"You bastard," she said under her breath. "Taking up with that tart, Abby Harris."

Gunn said nothing.

"Well, you picked sides, all right. I—I misjudged you. I thought there was some decency in you."

"Larrabee pays well."

"And the side benefits aren't bad either!"

"No, ma'am."

"You—you . . . I hope I never see you again!"

"I was on my way to see Debbie," he said quietly. "She doin' all right?"

"Yes, no thanks to you. Poor girl's eating her heart out. She trusted you. Her father trusted you."

"She at the hotel?"

"Yes. I tried to get her to stay with me, but she's independent. Do me a favor, Gunn. Get out of her life. Don't see her. You—you've hurt her enough already."

He tipped his hat and walked on without looking back. Across the street he saw Jake Early grinning. Gunn grinned back.

It was tough playing it this way, but it was the only chance he had to find out what he had to know. Gordo hadn't been around. The saddlebags had been returned and his money had still been in the coffee tin. It was still there. He didn't trust Abby. He had an eerie feeling just being with her. Knowing that Lorenzo Miller had been her lover and was now dead. Abby wasn't a tramp. She was just an unusual woman. She worked for Larrabee but was not attracted to him. Nor, apparently, did he look at her as other than an employee. Instead, Gunn learned that he had a widow he was sparking, off and on, and, once a month he took the stage up to Alburquerque, stayed for two or three days. Gunn didn't ask questions. He just listened. Gradually, some of the men had loosened up around him. When they were out back, smoking or taking a leak, they would talk. Mostly about women and sometimes about Larrabee.

Larrabee, he learned, had come from San Francisco. For a long time he had laid low, as Monica had told him, then he had suddenly come up with money. A lot of money. Apparently he had more of it, because he was gradually buying up most of the businesses along Main Street. He was angry that he couldn't buy the hotel. Couldn't find out who the owner was. Gunn had smiled at that. If he only knew, Monica's life wouldn't be worth a tin two-bit piece. And, he wanted to buy into the stage line, but had to step careful there. From all that Gunn could gather, he was as secretive as a widow-woman with a nest egg. There was only one reason a man like Larrabee had to be so careful. He was a wanted man!

While he knew he had never met Larrabee before, there was still something familiar about him.

Everytime he heard San Francisco mentioned, something clanged in his mind. A memory struggled to rise up and be noticed.

But Gunn had never been to San Francisco.

He had started to go there once, but had gotten sidetracked.

Now, he wished he had gone.

Still, there was some connection. It would come, in time. The best way to recall it was to forget about it.

Gunn knocked on the door to Debbie's room.

"Who is it?"

"Gunn."

The door opened. Debbie looked surprised to see him.

Not happy, though.

"I—I didn't think you'd have the nerve to come here," she said tautly.

"May I come in? I just wanted to see how you were doing."

She looked at him carefully. Gunn took off his hat, held it in front of him, working the brim with both hands, like a penitent peon come to confession.

"Come in," she said.

The woman in the chair rose up. Her face was dark with held-in anger.

"Julieta was just leaving. Thank you for coming by, Julieta. I'll see you tomorrow?"

Julieta swaggered up to Gunn, then turned to Debbie.

"I will stay now if you wish."

"No, it's all right. Gunn and I have some talking to do. Tomorrow."

"Tomorrow."

Julieta slammed the door hard, voicing her displeasure that Gunn was there.

Debbie set him a chair and he sat down. She sat on

the bed, some distance from him.

"I don't have anything to offer you," she said.

"I won't stay long. How are you?"

"You took your sweet time coming to find out."

So, it was going to be that way. He had expected as much. Even though he hadn't come to see Debbie, he had kept tabs on her. It was a small town. People talked. Gossipped. He knew that she had not gone to stay at Lorna's. Knew that the midwife came to see her every day. And Monica, too. Monica had not been on the desk when he'd come up. He'd known that. This was her day off, too, and that's why he had come now.

"I've been busy," he said.

"Yes, I know. Lorna told me. And Monica. I was shocked at first. Then I realized that you didn't owe me anything. In fact, I owe you more than I can repay."

"No, that's not the way it is," he said lamely.

"Oh really?" Her voice rose in pitch. "I suppose you think we can still be friends? Well, we can't! You're working for the man who killed my father! Who burned down my house! I hate you, Gunn! I hate you!"

"Please," he said. "I didn't come here to quarrel. I really am concerned about you."

"You're a traitor!" she shrieked. "Oh, how could you do this to me?" She put her head in her hands, started weeping.

He wanted to go to her, to comfort her. To tell her that he hadn't gone over to the other side.

But he couldn't.

She would tell Lorna or Monica and they would tell someone else and that would be the end of it.

He wanted to trust her, but he couldn't. He could trust no one until this was over.

He stood up, put his hat back on.

"I'm sorry, Debbie. I didn't want to hurt you. You've been through hell and I . . ."

"Just get out," she sobbed. "Just get out of my life . . ."

Her words rang in his ears as he made his way down the stairs and across the lobby. Lorna and Debbie both hated him. At least Debbie hadn't said anything about Abby. Maybe she didn't know. Lorna probably wouldn't have told her.

He had one more person to see and that was going to be the toughest.

Monica.

But that would have to wait until evening.

And no one could know about it.

He walked over to the Hog & Keg, went inside.

It was cool at the bar. The windows were all open and a fresh breeze aired the place out.

Larrabee, Jake and Gus were all sitting at a table. They beckoned for him to come over.

Gunn ordered a beer, carried it with him to the table. He scraped the chair sitting down.

"Good week, Gunn," said Larrabee, handing him an envelope. Gunn opened it. His pay. He stuck it in his gunbelt and smiled.

"Thanks," he said. "Easiest money I ever made."

"It's going to get tougher," said Jake.

"Never mind, Jake. I'll explain it all to Gunn." He

looked at Gunn, then, and drew out a pair of cigars.
He handed one over. Gunn took it. Larrabee lit both
of them after the ends were bit off, the tip wet down.

"What's on your mind, Larrabee?" Gunn asked as
the smoke bit at his throat and lungs.

"Call me Nat. Did you notice that English dude
that's been in here every night? Winning some high
stakes?"

Gunn had seen him. Not at his table, but at
another man's. Dearing's.

"I saw him. Proper gent. Tweed suit that must be
hotter'n Hades."

The men at the table laughed as one. Gus's face
was red from drink. He didn't say much. Jake looked
as if he'd been eating nails all morning.

"That's the one. Well, he's got a bad habit. Now, I
don't mind a man winning at my tables. But this, ah,
gentleman, who calls himself Wilbert Leffingwell, is
cleaning us out then going over to the Rio Queen
and losing all his winnings. Now that's what I call an
unfair distribution of profits. Wouldn't you?"

Gunn thought of his answer carefully. He knew he
was being put to some kind of test. He didn't like it.

"Man doesn't like to see his money go to the
competition," he said.

Larrabee laughed, slapped Gunn heartily on the
back.

"There, Jake, you see! My sentiments exactly.
Well, Gunn, we won't have to worry about his high
and mightiness Mister Leffingwell after tonight.
You see, Gordo has been on a little vacation and he's
anxious to use his muscles."

218

"Yeah," said Jake, grinning. "The crusher. He's going to wait for Leffingwhatever and break his fuggin' head."

"Tonight," said Larrabee. "After the bastard leaves the tables and heads for the Rio Queen. A little lesson for all concerned."

"Why are you telling me this?" Gunn asked.

"Because, I want you to pay attention. That's part of your job too. And, we have one for you. Not tonight. Two roughings up in one night would be suspicious. Don't you think? Gordo's not going to do anything illegal. Just scare the old gentleman a little bit. And we're going to do that to a lot of Lorna's customers."

Gunn saw it now. No killing. Just a little rough stuff to make Lorna's business suffer. Slick. And nothing she could do about it. He suspected that it had all happened before.

"What do you want me to do, Nat?" Gunn said the man's given name, hoping that his distaste was concealed.

"The man with the blue bandanna. You played with him a week ago at Baldy's table. He's another one. Give it a couple of days, then you work him over. Make sure he gets the message. Either he plays at the Hog & Keg or he doesn't play. Might be good to break a couple of fingers if he argues with you. There'll be a little extra sugar in your pay next week."

"Fine. If he comes back in, I'll tag him."

Gunn finished his beer, said he wanted to get some sleep. He stood up, and was about to leave when

219

Larrabee said something that socked him between the eyes. It was meant to be friendly, but in saying it Larrabee ticked off that bell in Gunn's brain.

"By the way, Gunn, you ever been to San Francisco?"

"No. Never did."

"Ran into a friend of yours once. If you're the same Gunn."

Larrabee's eyes narrowed. Gunn's senses prickled.

"Who would that be, Nat?"

"Soo Li. Pretty little Chinee gal. Talked about you right friendly. If you ever see her again, give her my regards."

"I don't know anyone by that name," said Gunn easily. "Pretty name. But, like I said, I've never been to 'Frisco."

It was hard to miss the smirk on Larrabee's face. Gunn saluted and left, knowing they would talk about him after he was gone.

Outside, he drew in a breath. Wondered if he'd pulled it off. Larrabee had been testing him, for sure. After a week, the man was probably convinced that Gunn was a nobody. Not the man he'd heard about. He had played it pretty close to the vest. Abby had tried to pump him about his past, but he hadn't told her much. None of it true. For all she knew, he was just a drifter. A down-on-his-luck straggler who drifted with the wind, like a tumbleweed. And that was the impression he had wanted to give Larrabee. The others had pried at him, too, and he'd led them all up a false trail.

Now, Larrabee had mentioned Soo Li.

And now he remembered. The last time he'd seen Soo Li was at Tres Piedras and Taos. But he'd met her long before. He had expressed surprise at how her English had improved. That's when she told him about a man she'd met in San Francisco who had helped her with her speech. But, that was not all.

Soo Li had said the same man had told her of a scheme he had, without outlining any of the details. He said he would soon be rich. He asked her to go away with him. Something about him had stunned her off, however. Her suspicions were confirmed when a Wells Fargo stage, carrying a lot of money, San Francisco money, had been robbed. All of the passengers, driver and guard, killed. It was a major scandal. None of the men had been captured. The strongbox had contained more than $100,000 in small bills. A fortune.

There were three men who robbed the stage. The man riding shotgun had lived long enough to give a description. And, he'd heard two names. Jack, or Jake. And Gus. The other man, the leader, had never spoken. But he was the one who had killed the two women passengers and an Army sergeant. In cold blood.

Soo Li said she had never seen the man again. But she told Gunn his name.

It wasn't Nathaniel Larrabee.

Not then.

In San Francisco, he'd used the name of Nelson Lawrence.

The same initials.

Now, Gunn knew the source of Larrabee's wealth.

Nathaniel Larrabee was Nelson Lawrence. Or vice versa.

And, he'd bet dollars to pesos that Gus Whitcomb and Jake Early had been the other two robbers of the Wells Fargo stage!

* * *

Gunn slipped along the backs of the buildings, keeping to the shadows.

There was a scud-cover of clouds masking the moon and stars, making it easier for him.

In his hand, he carried a spade. Purloined from the back of the Hog & Keg.

He didn't have much time.

There were other appointments he had to keep.

It was the only way.

He crept across the street, looked both ways.

It was clear.

Lights burned in Monica's windows. Good. She was home.

He stole across the street to the vacant lot. He hunched over, made his way to the stove.

In the dark, he felt for the right leg. Grunting, he put his shoulder to the stove, pushed it back two feet. Then, he began digging. Slowly, widening the hole, gently sloshing out the dirt. The spade struck something hard. Something metallic. Carefully, Gunn worked the spade around the object. More scraping. The box was where Caleb had said it would be.

Buried under the stove.

Gunn lifted it out, left the spade where it was.

222

Then, he walked across the street, went to Monica's back door. He knocked softly.

Monica opened the door.

Her face registered surprise.

"Let me in," Gunn whispered. "Quick!"

"Yes, come in," she said, still startled.

"Lock the door. Pull the shades."

In the living room, Gunn set the metal box on the floor. It was locked.

"What's going on?" she said. "I thought . . ."

"Never mind what you thought, Monica. Have you got a pry? A poker or something?"

She brought him a poker from the fireplace. She pulled all the shades.

Gunn pried the lid until the lock snapped. He opened the box. There, dusty and moldy, was the journal of Caleb Barnes.

"Is that . . . is that Caleb's journal?"

Gunn beamed.

"It is. Not a word, now. Want to read it with me?"

They sat on the couch. Gunn read a page, handed it to Monica.

It was all there. Caleb had found out about Nat Larrabee. A lot of the information had come from Lorenzo Miller, Monica's husband. Through his contacts, he had found out about Larrabee's past. His real name was Nelson Lawrence. And a woman had worked for Wells Fargo. She had been the one to set it all up. Had told Lawrence/Larrabee that the stage would be carrying that money.

Jake Early and Gus Whitcomb had been in on it, too.

"I—I never knew," said Monica. "Lonny never said a word . . ."

"He was probably a good detective. And Caleb was one hell of a writer. I'm sure that they both made an agreement to keep quiet until they had all the facts."

"But . . . but there's enough here to hang them. To hang them all!"

"No, Monica. Not all of them. Look. The journal's not finished. There's one missing piece."

"I—I don't understand."

"The woman. The one who worked at Wells Fargo. They were getting close. Too close. I think your husband was just about to find out who she was when Gordo killed him. She must have set him up, like she did the stage."

"But who . . . ?"

"A cold one, Monica. A woman with icewater in her veins."

Monica gasped. She looked at Gunn.

His jaw was set. His pale blue-gray eyes were like shining nickels in the lamplight.

"You know, don't you?"

He sucked in a breath.

"I know," he said. "I can't prove it, yet. But I know." He paused, looked at her, a tenderness in his eyes that melted her. "Hide this somewhere safe. I want Debbie to have it when it's all over. It ought to be worth some money to her. Wells Fargo has a reward out and the manuscript can be sold. I'm sure you and she will share the reward as survivors of the men who broke the case."

"But you . . ." she stammered.

Gunn stood up.

"I don't want anything except some hides. I'm going now. Don't go anywhere, or see anyone."

"What are you going to do?"

"I'm going to flush them out. Every damned one of them. Starting with Gordo."

Before Monica could say anything, Gunn was gone.

Monica sat there for a long time, shivering.

CHAPTER SEVENTEEN

Gordo waited in the shadows of the hotel across the street.

Lights blazed in the Hog & Keg. Laughter and music drifted on the night air.

He watched the batwing doors. A man came to the window, lit a match. The match went out. The man lit another match.

Gordo smiled.

That was the signal.

A few moments later, a man in a tweed suit came through the batwing doors. He preened himself for a moment, then crossed the street, headed for the Rio Queen. His derby hat was set at a jaunty angle.

"Psssst!" hissed Gordo from the shadows.

Wilbert Leffingwell paused.

"Come here," said Gordo.

"Eh wot?" asked Leffingwell. "I say . . ."

He drew close and Gordo shot out an arm. His fist crunched into the Englishman's face. The Englishman staggered back, withstanding the punch miraculously. Gordo waded after him, swinging. Leffingwell ducked, came up with a surprising uppercut that caught Gordo square on the chin. The blow staggered the rotund Mexican. Leffingwell danced away as Gordo roared with anger, tried to squeeze him in a bear hug.

"Run along, chap," breathed the Englishman. "Or I shall be forced to box your ears off."

Indeed, Leffingwell assumed a pugilist's stance, left arm outstretched, the right cocked close to his chest, both fists upraised.

Enraged by such behavior, Gordo rushed Leffingwell. His speed was deceptive. The Britisher was caught off guard. Gordo came in low, from the side. He didn't swing, but crashed into Wilbert with a solid body tackle, hurling the gentleman to the ground.

The air rushed out of the Englishman's lungs.

Gordo began hitting the man hard, slamming fists into his face as he sat atop him, crushing him.

"Hold it, Gordo!" said a voice behind him.

Gordo froze, whirled, his right hand suspended in mid-air.

"Who . . . ?"

"It's Gunn. Get off that man or I'll blow your brains out where you sit."

Gordo rose slowly, as the Englishman wriggled away.

"You sonofabitch, Gunn, I been waiting for you a long fucking time."

"Go for it, Gordo." Gunn stepped into the light, holstered his Colt. Gordo saw the movement, grinned wide. Leffingwell sat up blinked at what he saw. He slipped fingers inside his coat, but stopped when he saw the speed of Gordo's draw, and a split second later, Gunn's.

Gordo thought he had Gunn cold. His hand clasped the butt of his pistol. He felt the pistol tug free of the holster. Then, Gunn's hand streaked like a trout's shadow. The Colt was in his hand, bucking, spitting fire and deadly lead.

Gordo felt the first slug hit him in the gut. At first it was like a hot poker had been shoved through his belly, then something slammed into his spine, and he went numb below the waist. Then, a second shot, with his own pistol way off somewhere at the end of his arm weighing a long ton, and pain spreading across his chest for only a split second.

Gunn hammered back, triggered so fast Leffingwell's jaw dropped to his chest. The third shot from the Colt entered Gordo's skull, eyebrow high, and blew out the back of his head. A pink froth sprayed the air, the droplets shining in the light from the Hog & Keg.

"Englishman, get some legs under you," barked Gunn as a tail of smoke spewed from the barrel of his pistol. "This street's going to be a shooting gallery in about two seconds."

"By Jove, you've a point, sir!"

Gunn melted into the shadows as the doorway of the Hog & Keg became filled with heads silhouetted against the light. The Englishman dashed up the street toward the Rio Queen, running in the street instead of on the boardwalk, so that his fine boots made little sound.

Shouts filled the street. People peered out of the windows of the Hog & Keg.

Gunn ran in back of the hotel, appointments to keep.

In the street, Gordo was a huge hulk in a pool of blood, already gone to his Maker. Three clean holes in him. Gut, heart, head.

* * *

Gunn knew where Gus Whitcomb spent his early evenings. It was one of several things he had learned during his week of patient listening.

He didn't bother knocking on the flimsy door of the *jacal,* but kicked in the door.

Gus was putting the boots to the Mexican girl when Gunn burst inside the one-room adobe shack.

He rose up, naked, snaked a hand out for his pistol.

The girl, who wasn't more than twelve, screamed.

Gunn, his pistol loaded with fresh bullets, five of them, triggered the first shot. The bullet caught Gus square in his left eye, blew the pulpy orb clean through his skull, leaving an empty socket.

Gus grunted, rolled onto the floor, screaming in agony. Gunn shot twice more, the shots so close together they sounded almost as one. Gus twitched as his heart exploded in his chest. Twitched a last time as his intestines burst, filling the air with a foul stench.

"Get dressed and get out of here," Gunn said to the frightened girl.

And then, he was gone.

* * *

Jake Early couldn't stop his hand from shaking. He stood in Larrabee's office, his knees threatening to buckle.

"Godamnit, Nat, it's Gunn. First Gordo, and then Gus. Just like those rustlers up in Wyoming. Three bullets in each of 'em."

"Where is the sonofabitch?" Larrabee demanded.

"I don't aim to find out. Just give me a stake and let me ride on out. If you're smart, you'll do the same. That bastard is a-huntin' us. He means to gun us all down before mornin'."

Larrabee knew Jake was right. He had known it ever since they'd found Gordo shot up like that. And then the Mexican gal telling them about Gus when Nate Crumb brought her to the Hog & Keg. Jake had confirmed that kill. He had closed up the saloon. Crumb was watching the front door, Harve the back. It was spooky quiet.

"Think you can make it, Jake?"

"I can make it. Just give me a thousand."

"All right. Meet up in Roswell like we planned?"

"Yeah. Two, three days. When it quiets down. We can always come back after Gunn leaves."

Larrabee opened the safe, counted out a thousand dollars. He handed the money to Jake.

"Be careful, Nat."

"He's only one man."

"He's a devil."

Larrabee was glad to see Jake go. The man had gone to pieces on him. Well, he wasn't going to let Gunn rattle him. He heard the back door open and close. Harve said something to Jake and then it was quiet again.

Larrabee took money from the safe, put it in his vest. Then, he closed and locked the safe. He checked his pistol, spinning the cylinder. Satisfied, he holstered it, put the thong on the hammer ear. Then, he stooped down and opened the bottom drawer of his desk. Pulled out the sawed-off shotgun. He stuffed extra shotshells in his coat pockets, checked the shotgun by cracking it open at the breech. Loaded.

He walked back to see Harve.

"Call it a night," he said. "Lock up after I leave, will you, Harve?"

"Sure, boss." Harve carried a shotgun, too. Loaded with double ought buck in both barrels. It wasn't sawed off.

Larrabee walked through the empty saloon to the front door where Nate Crumb sat in a chair.

"Nate. I'm going now. You come along, back me up."

"Where to, boss?"

"Pay a call on Lorna Starr."

"What're you gonna do?"

"I'm going to kill her. She put that bastard up to this. I should have seen it a week ago. He wormed his way in here, but he was working for Lorna."

"That's what you figgered at first. How come you let him work here?"

"If you've got a fox in the henhouse, you close the door and keep him in there. I thought we could keep an eye on Gunn if he was right under our noses. I just didn't figure he'd move this fast, or this way."

"He must've found out something."

"Yeah, he must have."

The two men left. Inside the saloon, Harve started locking up, blowing out candles. He would sleep upstairs where he always did, but now he felt trapped.

* * *

Jake saddled his horse quickly, tied on his bedroll, led the animal out of the livery. He had been as quiet as he could, jumping at every sound, nevertheless.

He had one foot in the stirrup when Gunn walked out to him.

"Going somewhere, Jake?"

Jake's heart flew into his throat. His leg came down out of the stirrup. His boot heel hit the ground hard. He whirled, instinctively going into a crouch, hand thrusting down for the butt of his pistol.

Gunn shot him in the gut first.

Jake went to his knees, sobbing with pain. His pistol dangled from his right hand.

"You'll die slow, Jake. Like Caleb Barnes."

"No, Jesus. Gunn . . ."

Gunn kicked the man's pistol out of his hand, walked away, up the street. Behind him, Jake whined and tried to hold in the slick coil of intestines that writhed in his hands like snakes.

* * *

Larrabee heard the shot, froze. Behind him, Nate Crumb drew his pistol.

"What was that?"

"A shot, dammit," said Larrabee. he cocked the hammers of the sawed-off shotgun.

He listened for the other two shots.

Only silence.

He started to sweat.

"Come on," he grunted. "We'll have to skip the Rio Queen."

"Where we goin'?"

"You get three horses saddled, meet me at Abby's."

"We gonna run for it?"

"You're damned right, Nate. We're going to run like hell."

* * *

Gunn hoped his hunch was right.

He ran hard, crossing the street. He dashed between two buildings, then raced up the next street. No one saw him. He hit a stride and ran easily, on the balls of his feet, loading a fresh bullet into the cylinder of his Colt.

He went inside the adobe, took the stairs three at a time.

Abby's door was locked.

He knocked loudly.

The door opened.

Abby stood there, in a diaphanous negligee. He could see right through it.

She stared at him, backlit by the lamp in the parlor.

"I wondered if it would be you," she said softly.

"You were expecting Larrabee?"

"Eventually."

He stepped inside, closed the door. He didn't lock it. He took Abby's arm, led her into the living room.

He smelled brandy on her breath. The fumes were overpowering.

"When did you figure it out?"

"A while ago. Surprised?"

"No. I knew someone would, someday."

"You were the one who worked at Wells Fargo," he said. "Set the whole thing up."

"Yes."

"It's all over now."

"Is Nelson dead?"

"No. He'll be here."

"Don't kill him, please."

"You love him?"

"No. Don't you know who I am? Caleb couldn't figure it out, either. Nor Lorenzo. I guess it was the blonde hair. It's bleached. Lonny was getting close but I fooled him. Fooled them all."

Gunn realized she was drunk.

He looked at her carefully. At her eyes, her facial structure. He should have seen it before. He squinted, tried to imagine her hair dark. The mouth was the same, or almost.

234

"What name did you use at Wells Fargo?"

"Abigail Nelson. A good touch, don't you think?"

"What is it, really? Lawrence?"

Abby laughed, on the verge of hysteria.

"Yes. Abigail Lawrence."

"Larrabee's kid sister."

She laughed again, lurched to the sidebar where the brandy decanter glowed amber in the light. She poured herself a drink, downed it.

"He used you, Abby. Turned you into a plaything for men who wiped their boots on you."

"No, I did that. I was never any good, Gunn. Not until you came along. I had hoped we could . . ."

Footsteps pounded on the stairs.

Stopped.

Gunn turned, heard a challenging voice, strangely high-pitched, with an elusive accent. One he'd heard before.

Someone cursed.

Shots rang out. Two, three. Another.

The front door burst open.

Someone ran through the parlor.

Gunn heard a thud on the stairs. More footsteps.

Larrabee came into the room, the shotgun held level in his hands.

"I'm going to kill you, Gunn, if it's the last thing I do!"

Gunn crouched, his hand shooting to his pistol.

Abby rushed forward just as Larrabee pulled both triggers of the shotgun.

The deadly hail of lead caught Abby in the face and chest.

Her scream cut off as Gunn's pistol leaped into

his hand.

Larrabee looked at his sister in horror as the first bullet struck him in the chest. The second hit him in the belly, staggered him backwards.

Gunn shot him a third time, his anger causing a reflexive action of his trigger finger.

A man came into the room just as Larrabee fell backwards, a hole in his forehead.

"I say, guv'nor, bloody mess, what? I shot the other bloke. Couldn't catch up to this one."

"Who in hell are you?" Gunn asked, the smoke from his pistol stinging his nostrils.

"Leffingwell. Wilbert Leffingwell. With Wells Fargo. Been on this trail a bloody long while."

Gunn smiled.

Life was full of surprises.

* * *

The three women stood outside the livery as Gunn led the dun horse outside.

"Ladies," he said.

"We wish you would stay," said Lorna Starr.

Gunn patted Duke's neck, rubbed his muzzle.

"You'll have a good town before long," he said. "Maybe I'll come back someday."

"Thanks, Gunn," said Debbie. "For everything. I think I can finish my pa's book. Monica's going to help me."

"There is a reward coming from Wells Fargo," said Monica. "Part of it should be yours."

"Just spell my name right when you do your book," Gunn said, swinging up into the saddle. "Or

236

maybe you ought to just leave it out. I think Leffing-well can use some credit."

"Leffingwell offered you a job with Wells Fargo," said Lorna.

"I know. Too dull."

Gunn saluted, touched his spurs to Duke's flanks. The three women waved as the horse trotted away.

"Are you coming back soon?" asked Lorna, rushing up to him impulsively, leaving the other two women standing alone. She touched his leg with delicate hands. "I really want you to."

She ran alongside his horse, pressed something into his hand.

Gunn looked into her eyes. Saw the fire there. The yearning.

"I'd like to come back. To see you, especially."

"I'll be waiting," she said, blowing him a kiss. He waved, stepped up Duke's pace.

He looked back. The three women were still waving at him. He raised a hand. To Lorna, he blew an answering kiss.

She would understand.

For Lorna's sake, he would be back. He opened his hand, looked at the object she had put there.

A small round snuffbox.

He opened it.

Inside, was a lock of hair. Tied with a dainty yellow ribbon. He held it up to the sun. It shone like copper, like delicate gold.

Smiling, he put the lock back in the box, closed it up. Then he tucked the box into the pocket of his buckskin shirt. Next to his heart.

It was a good day for riding. A good day to think about the women of Socorro. He would always remember them.

Always.

THE END

WORLD WAR II
FROM THE GERMAN POINT OF VIEW

SEA WOLF #1: STEEL SHARK   (755, $2.25)
by Bruno Krauss

The first in a gripping new WWII series about the U-boat war waged in the bitter depths of the world's oceans! Hitler's crack submarine, the U-42, stalks a British destroyer in a mission that earns ruthless, ambitious Baldur Wolz the title of "Sea Wolf"!

SEA WOLF #2: SHARK NORTH   (782, $2.25)
by Bruno Krauss

The Fuhrer himself orders Baldur Wolz to land a civilian on the deserted coast of Norway. It is winter, 1940, when the U-boat prowls along a fjord in a mission that could be destroyed with each passing moment!

SEA WOLF #3: SHARK PACK   (817, $2.25)
by Bruno Krauss

Britain is the next target for the Third Reich, and Baldur Wolz is determined to claim that victory! The killing season opens and the Sea Wolf vows to gain more sinkings than any other sub in the Nazi navy . . .

SEA WOLF #4: SHARK HUNT   (833, $2.25)
by Bruno Krauss

A deadly accident leaves Baldur Wolz adrift in the Atlantic, and the Sea Wolf faces the greatest challenge of his life—and maybe the last!

Available wherever paperbacks are sold, or order direct from the Publisher. Send cover price plus 50¢ per copy for mailing and handling to Zebra Books, 475 Park Avenue South, New York, N.Y. 10016. DO NOT SEND CASH.